P9-BZC-907

It felt so good to be using skills that had been dormant for so long. When was the last time she'd actually fought someone—and showed her true mettle? Five years ago? Six years? Loki would be so proud if he could see her now. She straightened as Gaia sagged and futilely tried to suck in breath. Ella chuckled. Yes . . . pummeling her foster daughter filled her with a satisfaction she hadn't experienced in far too long. Of course, it was nothing compared to the euphoria of knowing that she had crushed Gaia's will, that she had *destroyed* Gaia—that she had stolen the one heart Gaia prized above all others.

That was the real triumph. And Ella would savor it.

Don't miss any books in this thrilling series:

FEARLESS™

Available from POCKET PULSE

For orders other than by individual consumers, Pocket Books grants a discount on the purchase of **10 or more** copies of single titles for special markets or premium use. For further details, please write to the Vice-President of Special Markets, Pocket Books, 1260 Avenue of the Americas, New York, NY 10020–1586, 8th Floor.

For information on how individual consumers can place orders, please write to Mail Order Department, Simon & Schuster Inc., 100 Front Street, Riverside, NJ 08075.

FEARLESS™

TRUST

FRANCINE PASCAL

POCKET PULSE
New York   London   Toronto   Sydney   Singapore

To Jordan Adler

The sale of this book without its cover is unauthorized. If you purchased this book without a cover, you should be aware that it was reported to the publisher as "unsold and destroyed." Neither the author nor the publisher has received payment for the sale of this "stripped book."

This book is a work of fiction. Names, characters, places, and incidents are either products of the author's imagination or are used fictitiously. Any resemblance to actual events or locales or persons, living or dead, is entirely coincidental.

An *Original* Publication *of* POCKET BOOKS

 POCKET PULSE, published by
Pocket Books, a division of Simon & Schuster, Inc.
1230 Avenue of the Americas, New York, NY 10020

 Produced by 17th Street Productions,
an Alloy Online, Inc. company
33 West 17th Street
New York, NY 10011

Copyright © 2000 by Francine Pascal

Cover art copyright © 2000 by 17th Street Productions,
an Alloy Online, Inc. company.
Cover photography by St. Denis. Cover design by Mike Rivilis.

All rights reserved, including the right to reproduce this book or portions thereof in any form whatsoever. For information address 17th Street Productions, 33 West 17th Street, New York, NY 10011, or Pocket Books, 1230 Avenue of the Americas, New York, NY 10020.

ISBN: 0-671-03952-0

First Pocket Pulse Paperback printing August 2000

10 9 8 7 6 5 4 3 2 1

Fearless™ is a trademark of Francine Pascal.
POCKET PULSE and colophon are trademarks of Simon & Schuster, Inc.

Printed in the U.S.A.

TRUST

TRUST

Sam and Ella.

Sam Moon: The only guy I've ever desired.

Ella Niven: The evil witch who poses as my stepmother.

The two of them . . . together.

A part of me still refuses to believe it. True, I always knew that Ella was twisted. I always knew that behind the designer clothes and stupid façade lurked a schemer who was playing her husband for a chump. I even suspected that she was having an affair. Or something bad. Nobody's *that* vacant.

But never could I have possibly imagined that she was cheating on George with *Sam*.

And you know what the real kicker is? I actually feel sorry for Heather Gannis. I do. After all, Sam is still supposedly going out with Heather. I used to hate her for that. Okay, I hated her for a bunch of other stuff, too. But I remember thinking about Sam and Heather together—no, scratch that—*seeing* Sam and Heather together, in bed . . . actually, forget it. No point in rehashing the past. Even now it turns my stomach. But at least it makes *sense*. At least I can understand it. Sam and Heather are pretty much the same age. They hang out in the same social scene. They're both smart, attractive, whatever . . . blah, blah, blah. People wouldn't give them a second glance even if they were making out in the middle of Broadway.

On the other hand, somebody would probably look twice at a college kid who was tongue wrestling with a thirty-something bimbo. Especially if said bimbo dresses like a teenage hooker.

I guess the biggest question is this: How the hell did it even *happen?* How did they meet? Where? When? I've been through a thousand scenarios over and over again, and the only one that seems even remotely plausible is that Sam sought out Ella on purpose. Or vice versa. Either way, it doesn't really matter. What matters is that it was a deliberate act. Somehow, for some reason, Sam and Ella got it into their heads that they had to humiliate me, that they had to drive the final nail into the coffin of my already miserable life.

And they succeeded.

I will say this, though: Sneaking into Sam's room and reading the e-mail Ella sent him was strangely liberating. If you truly have nothing to lose, then you are truly free—in the most real sense of the word.

Yes, on one level they destroyed me. But they also opened a new door. They *changed* me. Because now I don't care about using my special gifts (fearlessness, expertise in a variety of martial arts, and near perfect marksmanship) just to kick the asses of scumbags who prey on the weak and innocent.

No. Now I'm going to use those gifts for revenge.

And I'm looking forward to it.

Luckily it was one of those rare moments when she felt blessed to be fearless. step—
Because she knew monster she should be terrified. She was losing this fight.

NOW I KNOW WHAT AN ANIMAL FEELS like. An animal stalking its prey.

The Shattering of Bones

Gaia Moore paced back and forth across the narrow foyer, staring at the front door. Every muscle was tensed in a state of readiness. Yes . . . she was like a tiger. Or a wolf. Her blue eyes were slits behind a shroud of tangled blond hair. Her sneakers barely made a sound on the worn strip of carpet. Her heart pounded in near perfect rhythm to the ticking grandfather clock. The Nivens' brownstone was cold and dark, but her skin felt very hot. She'd deliberately left the lights off. She didn't want Ella to know that anyone was home. She wanted to catch Ella completely by surprise—because as every black belt knew, surprise was the key to a quick defeat.

Not that Gaia imagined she would have any problems beating the shit out of her foster mother. But still, one could never be too careful—

There was a click, and Gaia froze.

Her eyes zeroed in on the front doorknob. It was turning. *This is it.* She held her breath. She could see Ella's silhouette through the panes of frosted glass—a dark figure against the glare of afternoon winter sunlight.

The stepmonster was home.

Ella pushed open the door, fumbling with a bunch of paper bags—no doubt filled with miniskirts or lingerie from some overpriced designer store that catered to women about ten years younger than she was. But Gaia's attention wasn't focused on Ella's belongings. No . . . her gaze remained pinned to Ella's vacant green eyes.

All at once, Ella flinched.

The door slammed shut behind her. She stiffened and shot Gaia a baffled stare, frowning. Her bags dropped to the floor.

"What are you doing here?" Ella spat. "Why aren't you in school—"

"Does George know you sleep around?" Gaia interrupted. She was shocked at the sound of her own voice. It was cold, hoarse—the voice of a stranger.

Ella blinked. For an instant a fleeting smile crossed her face. Then she sighed and began unwrapping her scarf. "Excuse me?" she said.

"You heard me," Gaia croaked.

"Does George know I sleep around?" Ella echoed, pursing her collagen-enhanced lips. Her tone was flat, impossible to read. She shrugged gracefully out of her short fur jacket and crossed to the front hall closet, stepping within inches of Gaia's clenched fists. "You know, that's a pretty offensive accusation, Gaia. Even for you."

"Not half as offensive as your having sex with Sam Moon," Gaia hissed. Her voice shook with rage. Ella was so close. Gaia felt her legs dipping into a combat stance, as if acting of their own volition: muscles coiled, feet flat, knees bent. Her body was preparing itself to fight.

Ella just shook her head. With her back turned, she hung up her coat—almost as if she were taunting Gaia, daring her to strike. Then she closed the closet door and glanced over her shoulder. A satisfied grin slowly spread across her face.

"Boys will be boys," she murmured.

Gaia gaped at her. For a moment her body went slack. She couldn't believe it. Ella wasn't even trying to deny that the affair had taken place. This was crazy. Whatever Gaia had been expecting, it wasn't this blatant, icy, arrogant *up yours*. Usually when Gaia caught Ella in a lie, the woman would scream or spew threats—and her face would twist with fear and rage.

But Ella didn't even look troubled. She met Gaia's gaze head-on. Gaia thought she had seen every single mask of deception that Ella had ever worn: a thousand different faces for a thousand different situations. But this victorious expression was one Gaia had never seen before . . . which made it all the more disturbing.

"What's the matter?" Ella whispered.

Gaia swallowed. Fizzy threads of adrenaline began to snake through her veins. "You, you—you *bitch*," she stammered, unable to form a coherent thought through the haze of anger.

"Why don't you just face what's really bothering you?" Ella asked matter-of-factly. She cocked her head and lowered her voice. "It's not that I cheated on George. That's for damn sure. So you can drop the high-and-mighty act. What's bothering you is that Sam Moon made love to me. To *me*," she repeated. Her smile widened.

Gaia's entire body now hummed with a pulsating electric energy. Various kung fu and karate techniques whirled through her mind. She would choose the most painful form of attack. Ella's self-involved little rant would end in the shattering of bones. . . .

"I know what he tastes like," Ella continued, whispering. "I know what he feels like. What he smells like. I know what sounds he makes—"

"*Hai!*" Gaia cried, lashing out with a right jump kick.

But to Gaia's utter shock, Ella jumped backward and expertly dodged the strike.

Gaia caught a glimpse of a strange, amused smirk on Ella's face. *What the hell?* Gaia bit her lip. But there was no time to ask herself questions. *Focus!* she savagely screamed at herself. Ella had just gotten lucky. That was all. Her luck wouldn't last, though. Gaia had telegraphed that first kick. She wouldn't make the same mistake twice. . . .

The next instant Gaia feinted with her left hand—then arced her right fist hard into Ella's ribs. There was a satisfying thunk and a sharp intake of breath, and Ella quit smiling. But before Gaia had a chance to follow through, Ella spun in a circle. She was a blur of arms and legs. Her right hand darted out and seized Gaia's left forearm, as quickly as a cobra's pouncing on a mouse.

"Hey!" Gaia protested. "What—"

Before Gaia knew it, she found herself being flung to the ground. The back of her head struck the floor with a sickening crack. A white flash exploded in front of her eyes. *Shit.* Luckily it was one of those rare moments when she felt blessed to be fearless. Because she knew she should be terrified. She was losing this fight. To *Ella.*

But all she felt was a cool, detached numbness. And pain.

Get up, an instinctive voice commanded.

She rolled—a fraction of a second before Ella kicked at her head—then sprang to her feet. Her breath came fast. Instantly she assessed the natural advantages she had: She was taller than Ella; she had longer arms and legs. She was also stronger, but she knew that mere strength could work against a person in combat.

Keeping her left fist close to her body, she punched with her right and caught Ella on the side of the head, feeling the hard skull beneath her knuckles. But Ella punched simultaneously: a left. Gaia blocked it and tried to sweep Ella's feet out from under her. Ella nimbly sidestepped the kick, then aimed a left-right-left combination that whistled past Gaia's cheekbone with an audible *whoosh*.

"You can fight," Gaia whispered out loud.

She stepped back. Something else was at work here. Yes. A terrible realization was creeping through her mind: This stupid bimbo was trained in martial arts. There was no doubt about it: Ella knew karate, kung fu, probably jujitsu as well. Her reflexes were perfectly honed. Underneath her soft-looking, hyperfeminine curves lay steel-hard muscles. Which meant that Ella wasn't a bimbo at all. Of course, Gaia had recently come to suspect that Ella was smarter than she pretended to be—but she'd never once imagined that Ella had been hiding abilities like *these*.

Ella smiled again, clearly sensing Gaia's bewilderment.

"Who are you?" Gaia found herself asking.

Instead of answering, Ella lunged forward with a barrage of chops and sidekicks. Gaia backtracked down the shadowy hall, blocking each successive strike. Ella's speed and accuracy were astonishing. And the brutal style of her attack betrayed a demonic viciousness Gaia had never seen before in an opponent—not even in the man who had killed Mary or that other guy who had attacked her in the park a few nights ago. . . .

"Who *are* you?" Gaia grunted again.

"You know who I am," Ella whispered. "I'm the woman Sam loves."

IT WAS A DISTINCT PLEASURE WATCHING

this spoiled brat's face dissolve under a crushing wave of pain. *Poor, poor Gaia,* Ella thought. *The truth hurts, doesn't it?*

She allowed herself another little smirk. Yes, with those last words, she knew she had delivered a blow far more powerful than any karate technique.

Leaky Inflatable Doll

Gaia's focus faltered for an instant, just as Ella knew it would. Almost instantaneously Ella launched a powerful side kick that landed squarely in Gaia's rock-hard solar plexus and knocked the oversized freak off her feet.

Ahh. That just about did it.

It felt so good to be using skills that had been

dormant for so long. When was the last time she'd actually fought someone—and showed her true mettle? Five years ago? Six years? Loki would be so proud if he could see her now. She straightened as Gaia sagged and futilely tried to suck in breath. Ella chuckled. Yes .. . pummeling her foster daughter filled her with a satisfaction she hadn't experienced in far too long. Of course, it was nothing compared to the euphoria of knowing that she had crushed Gaia's will, that she had *destroyed* Gaia—that she had stolen the one heart Gaia prized above all others.

That was the real triumph. And Ella would savor it.

As Gaia slumped against the wallpaper, Ella moved forward, a predator's grin on her face. It was time to end this little dance. But then she hesitated. Gaia was recovering. By now most adversaries would be out cold or begging pathetically for mercy . . . but not this one. Incredibly, Gaia was grunting and forcing herself upright. Ella had to hand it to the girl: She was strong.

"You shouldn't prolong this," Ella murmured. "You'll only hurt yourself more."

Gaia blinked, grimacing and clutching her stomach. "You . . . didn't . . . answer my question," she gasped breathlessly.

Ella laughed. "Oh, yes, I did."

"I don't believe you. You're lying—"

The front door burst open.

13

Ella whirled. *George!*

Not good. Ella swallowed. How much had her wimp of a so-called husband seen? He stood there for a moment in the open doorway, bundled in his overcoat and scarf, his haggard face twisting in confusion.

A bitter wind swept through the house. Ella remained perfectly rigid.

"Gaia?" George asked, his gaze darting between the two of them. "What's going on?"

"I came home and found that Gaia had skipped school," Ella stated in a clipped voice. Her answer was firm, authoritative. And it was the truth. Five years of experience in playing this charade with George had taught her that telling the truth (as much as possible, anyway) was always the best course of action. George might be blind to certain matters—like the fact that Ella was only *pretending* to be his wife—but he was surprisingly insightful about others. One didn't work for the CIA for thirty years and not learn how to detect *some* lies.

George closed the door behind him. His rheumy eyes remained fixed on Gaia. "Why aren't you in school?" he asked softly, sniffling from the cold.

"I . . . I . . ." Gaia shot a quick stare at Ella, then scrambled up the stairs.

"Gaia!" George yelled.

But there was no answer. Ella bit her lip to keep

from smiling. Gaia could barely make it to the top floor. Judging from the clumsy thumping of her feet, she was practically *dragging* herself up the last flight of stairs. Which meant that Ella had hurt her. And probably scared her, too—despite Loki's ridiculous assertions that Gaia was incapable of being afraid. Which also probably meant that the girl would keep quiet about their little . . . encounter.

"What on earth is going on?" George barked.

Ella shrugged calmly, then crossed the hall and turned on the light. "I have no idea. Like I said, Gaia was here when I got home."

George exhaled deeply and bowed his head. For a moment Ella almost felt sorry for him. He looked so listless and empty—like an inflatable doll that had sprung a leak. But pity only went so far. It certainly didn't detract from the intoxication of Gaia's defeat.

"We're falling apart," he muttered. "This house . . . this family isn't working. Nothing is working."

Ella regarded him closely. His words were true. But maybe she could take advantage of his fragile state. Loki was constantly demanding that she be more of a partner to George, that she play her role with more dedication. Now would be a perfect time to offer George solace. To reach out to him. To be a loving wife. Now would be a perfect time to prove to him that his ridiculous theories about her having an affair were completely unfounded.

15

And then today's victory would be complete.

She approached him and began unbuttoning his coat.

His head snapped up. "Wha-What are you doing?" he stammered.

"Helping you to relax," she whispered. "Come on. Get out of this stuff and go into the living room. We'll light a fire."

"What about Gaia?" he croaked, glancing over her shoulder at the stairwell. "Shouldn't one of us go up there and talk to her—"

"Shhh," Ella whispered gently, cutting him off in midsentence. "We'll talk to her later. It's too late for her to go back to school today. You need to unwind a little bit. You need to relax. Then we'll talk to Gaia, okay? I promise."

He opened his mouth, then closed it. His shoulders sagged.

Good, Ella thought as she slipped his coat off his shoulders and unwrapped his scarf. He didn't try to stop her. He'd surrendered. The plan was already working. A little wine, a roaring fire, some quiet intimacy . . . soon the day's troubles would melt away.

His coat fell to the floor, but he didn't stoop to pick it up. She reached out and caressed his face. *Yes . . . this is just what you need.* She ran her long, red fingernails through his thinning gray hair. She had no intention

16

of letting him talk to Gaia later, of course—but after she showed George an afternoon he'd never forget, he wouldn't want to. She was sure of it.

Absolutely Nobody

GAIA'S EYELIDS FLUTTERED OPEN. AT first she wasn't sure where she was. She was staring into a sea of fuzzy whiteness. There was something hard pressing against her back—

And then she remembered.

Ella had pretty much beaten her senseless.

So she must have passed out—the way she always did after a fight. Yup. Well, this was just perfect, wasn't it? She'd keeled over in her own house. (No, not her house; definitely not *her* house—as Ella was so fond of reminding her.) Once more her internal battery pack had run out. She was like the opposite of that little bunny from those commercials, the one that never stopped. She *couldn't* keep going. The exertion of combat had left her utterly drained, the way it always did.

And now she was sprawled on the hallway floor in

front of her bedroom. The fuzzy whiteness was the ceiling.

Gaia took a deep breath and sat up, hugging her knees against her chest. She shivered. These old houses never stayed warm enough during the winter.

A dull ache lodged itself in her stomach—and it wasn't because Ella had hit her there. No, it was because she felt so alone . . . more alone than she ever had in the four months since she'd come to New York City. The loneliness was a shroud, a blanket that smothered her. Not only did she hate her foster mother, but her foster mother hated *her*—with a far greater intensity than Gaia had ever suspected. And Gaia had no idea why. It wasn't because she'd skipped school.

Gaia's throat tightened. Her fists clenched. Whoever her foster mother really was, she was powerful. And dangerous. Deadly, in fact. Gaia's breath came hard and fast. Her stomach was clenched and roiling. There was a bitter taste in her mouth. Did Sam know Ella's true identity? Was *that* why he was attracted to her? Because Ella was such a badass? Because she destroyed every life she came in contact with, including the life of her poor, clueless, pitiful husband—

Stop it! She forced her fists to uncurl. She wouldn't think about Sam. For a moment she sat still, listening for any sounds of George and Ella downstairs. But there was nothing.

Gaia shook her head. Who *was* Ella? The question refused to go away. It gnawed at her relentlessly, torturing her. Where had she come from? Why was she with George? Gaia needed answers. She needed to talk to somebody about this. . . .

Ed. Of course.

She jumped to her feet.

But as quickly as the thought darted into her mind, she realized that talking to Ed was out of the question. She was barely *speaking* to Ed. In fact, she was downright pissed off at him. This very morning he had showed up at her house (uninvited) and made *her* feel guilty because *he* had suddenly decided to start hanging out with Heather Gannis again.

Whatever. There was no point in driving herself crazy about Ed Fargo—not on top of all her other problems. If Ed wanted to hang out with Heather, that was *his* loss.

So who could she talk to?

She loitered for a moment in her bedroom doorway. Her thoughts drew a rapid series of blanks. There was nobody. Absolutely nobody. Ed was fast becoming a stranger. . . . Mary Moss (the only true friend she'd made since she'd arrived in this hellish city) had been murdered at the hands of

19

Skizz's cronies. . . . She didn't have a father or mother. . . . Even her old friend Ivy had fallen out of touch. She was truly isolated. Cut off from everyone and everything—

Wait a second.

Unconsciously her hand dug into the front pocket of her cargo pants. Her fingers brushed against a small card. It was still there. Of course it was; she hadn't washed these pants in over two weeks.

She pulled out the white piece of cardboard and stared down at the ten neatly printed digits. Her uncle's phone number.

Uncle Oliver.

"We live in a dangerous world," he'd told her in the park this past Saturday, when he'd crept up on her— appearing out of nowhere and disappearing just as fast. *"And time is short."*

At first she'd been angry at his deliberate vagueness, at the creepy way he'd chosen to confront her after having kept himself hidden for so long. But now a thought was dawning on her: Did he somehow know about Ella? Was that the danger he was talking about? It wouldn't be that hard to believe. He seemed to know a lot about Gaia . . . a lot about everything, in fact. Maybe he ran in the same shadowy world as her father had—a world of deception and false identities and secrets only a select few knew. She wouldn't be surprised.

"This is my contact information. Use it anytime you feel the need."

Well, she certainly felt the need now. Her foster mother was a deadly sociopath. There was nowhere Gaia could run. For all intents and purposes, she was trapped in this house. And what if George hadn't come home and interrupted their fight? Would Ella have just finished her off? It was a distinct possibility. Gaia had never come that close to losing. Her very *life* could be in danger. Maybe it always had been in danger.

All of a sudden Gaia was sure that Oliver *did* know about Ella.

Without another moment's hesitation she strode into her bedroom and picked up the phone on her night table, then punched in the numbers. They began with 917.

After one ring there was a click. "Yes?"

Gaia's throat caught. The voice was so much like her father's: deep and resonant, but somehow soothing at the same time. She could hear the muffled sounds of traffic in the background.

"Um . . . Oliver?" she croaked. It was the first time she'd ever said his name out loud. The syllables sounded odd coming from her lips.

"Gaia," he whispered. "I was hoping you would call."

She swallowed. Her insides tensed. She had no idea what she was feeling right now—other than lost, adrift in a sea of bewildering emotions. "Can I see you?" she heard herself ask.

"Of course," he replied. "Let's have dinner Friday night. Meet me at Compagno's. It's a restaurant in Little Italy, on Mulberry Street. Eight o'clock."

Gaia opened her mouth to say something else, but the line went dead.

She blinked. That was it. She was going to see her uncle. She was going to reach out to this enigmatic man . . . this man who didn't *ask* her if she was free Friday night, this man who simply instructed her what to do, then hung up. His tone hadn't exactly been cold, but still—there was something sort of rude about how he'd handled her call. As if it were business. Not a family matter.

On the other hand, he probably *knew* that she didn't have other plans. He probably knew she was having a crisis. Why else would she have contacted him?

But then, shouldn't he have asked what was wrong? He was her uncle, after all. Her blood . . .

She supposed she could always blow him off.

No. Even as she considered this option, she knew deep down that she didn't have a choice. He was all she had.

The first time I ever met Gaia Moore, she was hateful and rude to me. So of course, I fell in love with her. That's just the way I am. Stupid. Call it love at first snarl. Certainly lust. My theory used to be that if you looked up the word *fine* in the dictionary, you'd see Gaia's picture. She's tall, close to five-nine is my guess, with long, blond hair to the middle of her back. Perfect skin, big eyes that change color from sky blue to the shade of ocean water during a storm . . .

Oops. Sorry. I'm forgetting myself. That happens sometimes.

The point is, I've had the hots for Gaia for about four months now. Actually, "hots" is an understatement. More like "infernos." I used to think about her pretty much every single second while I was awake and most of the seconds while I was asleep, too. Now it's maybe every other second. But it's still a lot.

The only bad part of this whole scenario is that she doesn't feel the same way.

Incredibly, though, it isn't because I'm in a wheelchair. I get the feeling with Gaia that a little thing like paraplegism wouldn't stop her from being attracted to someone. She's way more sophisticated than that. No, what has stopped her is someone called Sam Moon. She loves him. Wants him. Wants to go to bed with him.

And how do I know all this? Because she told me.

Right. Pay attention here.

Where it gets sticky is that Sam is dating Heather Gannis. Who is Gaia's worst enemy. And my ex-girlfriend. And now (possibly) my girlfriend again.

I know, I know—that doesn't make any sense. I can't figure it out, either. All I know is that Heather and I made out in a stor-age room in the Plaza Hotel (it would take *way* too long to

explain the circumstances here),
and ever since then, I've felt
like I could just jump out of my
wheelchair and run a marathon.
I've actually been *happy*.

There's only one little problem. Two, really. Heather still
hasn't officially dumped Sam, and
I'm still secretly in love with
Gaia.

But I've come to accept the
fact that Gaia is not about to
fall in love with me. Actually, I
don't even know if she likes me
anymore, even as a friend. And if
she ever found out about *everything* that went down between
Heather and me, she'd probably
never want to talk to me again.

So where does that leave me?

If I pursue this thing with
Heather (I know *thing* is a lame
word, but there's really no other
word that can accurately describe
the totally bizarre state of
affairs), I'll have a chance at
true happiness. She's perfect for
me. I've always known that, even

when she dumped me. She's one of
the few people who truly *under-
stands* me. And most important,
we're friends—above everything
else.

But if I *do* pursue this thing
with Heather, odds are about
ninety-nine to one that I'll lose
Gaia Moore forever.

Life has a funny way of suck-
ing, doesn't it?

There was something so surreal about the moment—as if he were acting out the **sweet pitch blackness** choreography of a well-rehearsed, recurring dream.

MOST FRIDAY NIGHTS ED FARGO

Tidal Wave

usually found himself following the same routine: (1) Pray that his parents would go out and leave him alone. (2) Watch TV and surf the web. (3) Call Gaia.

Yes, it was lame. It was pathetic, in fact—if you looked at it from the point of view of his former skate pals, who spent most Friday nights roaming the city and hopping from party to party. But Ed had lost his urge to explore the nightlife the day he'd lost the ability to use his legs. Unfortunately, nightlife and walking pretty much went hand in hand.

Still, he didn't mind being a hermit. The new Friday night routine was *comforting*, in a weird kind of way. It was comforting knowing that Gaia Moore was safe. When he was talking on the phone with her, he could be fairly certain that she wasn't out getting into trouble, or kicking people's asses . . . or worse. In fact, he used to spend *every* night on the phone with her for that exact reason. Well, also because he was in love with her. And also because it gave him something to do while he made milk shakes.

Ed leaned back in his wheelchair and stared at the phone on his desk. His eyes darted to the clock. It was almost eight. Usually by now he'd be chatting with Gaia, trading stupid one-liners and generally ragging on each others' lives.

Too bad he hadn't spoken to her since Monday.

The way things were looking, he could probably just toss that old Friday night routine right out the window. For all he knew, Gaia had left town. Or gotten thrown in jail. Or died. Ed wasn't prone to melodrama. No. Any of these scenarios was perfectly plausible. He hadn't even seen her in school for most of the week. And when he had, she'd made a very obvious and deliberate effort to avoid him.

He swallowed, debating whether or not to send her an e-mail. The little screen saver goldfish swam past him on his computer monitor. He reached for his mouse, but then his hand flopped down at his side. He couldn't do it. He couldn't bring himself to make the first move at reestablishing their friendship. Things were just too weird between them—and he had no idea why.

What the hell had *happened*, anyway?

He frowned, pushing himself away from his desk. Gaia had been pissed about the fact that he had been hanging out a lot with Heather . . . but still, she should have gotten over it. So what if Gaia hated Heather? For one thing, Gaia knew that Heather's sister was in the hospital, on the verge of death from a bout with anorexia. So she knew that Ed was *consoling* Heather. And for another thing, Gaia *didn't* know that Ed and Heather had shared a clandestine kiss on Sunday night. She never would, either. Unless she had

29

somehow found out. He swallowed again. No, that was impossible—

Brrring!

Ed jerked. The phone was ringing. He held his breath. Maybe that was her right now. Maybe they could end this foolishness once and for all and start being friends again. He leaned forward and snatched up the phone before the second ring.

"Hello?"

"Whatcha doing?"

Ed sighed. It wasn't Gaia. It was Heather.

But miraculously, after a split second or so, his initial disappointment faded. Yeah . . . in fact, he was *relieved* that Heather was on the phone. Wasn't he? Sure. Screw Gaia. He had better things to do than obsess over her. Heather was the one he could talk to—without any awkwardness or expectation. He cradled the phone more firmly between his ear and shoulder and smiled.

"Hello? Ed? Are you there?"

"Yeah, yeah," he said quickly. "Sorry. I'm just a little spaced out."

"I know what you mean," she said wryly. "That Friday night television lineup has the same effect on me, too."

Ed laughed. "I'll have you know, I was doing homework," he lied. He didn't want to sound like he was just sitting around, staring at the phone, waiting for Gaia to call. Or maybe he just didn't want to admit it to himself. He *definitely* didn't want to admit it to Heather.

"Homework on a Friday?" Heather mused. "Gosh, you're more deprived than I thought. Or is it depraved? What word am I looking for?"

"Very funny," Ed said with a smirk. "How about you? What are you up to? Besides heckling me, that is."

"I'm bored," said Heather easily, but didn't elaborate.

"Want to come over?" he found himself offering. The question popped out of his mouth before he even knew he wanted to extend the invitation. But he didn't regret it. He was lonely. "Watch a movie or something?"

"I'll be right there," she said, very softly.

Click.

Ed blinked. A strange warm tingle was moving from just above the base of his spine up to his neck. His heart started beating a fraction faster. She'd hung up . . . the way she used to hang up back when they were a couple, back before the accident—when he would call and she would rush over in an instant. He slowly replaced the phone in its cradle. For a moment he had a hard time catching his breath. Memories of Sunday rushed over him like a tidal wave, smothering him. Memories of that sweet pitch blackness, of the way Heather had reached out for him and smothered his lips with her own . . .

He smiled. Maybe his old Friday night routine had been flushed down the toilet. Whatever. If Heather's call was any indication of how a new routine might be shaping up, then he was all for a change.

THIS WAS IT. THE BIG MOMENT.

Gaia slammed the door to her bedroom, then stopped short at the top of the stairs. Maybe she should—check her appearance?

She hesitated, uncharacteristically unsure of herself. Usually when it was time to go out, she went out. But tonight was different. Tonight she would be sitting and sharing a meal with a blood relative—her uncle Oliver. Her father's brother. The man who had exploded into her life (once again) out of nowhere and at the time she needed somebody the most. It was a major event. So maybe she should . . . try to look nice? She didn't know if this was the kind of restaurant where people dressed up. She had a feeling it was. Her uncle seemed like a formal kind of guy.

Oh, well. At least her sweater didn't have any

holes in it. And her pants were reasonably clean and pressed.

After glancing down at herself and smoothing a few wrinkles, she darted into the bathroom and peered into the mirror over the sink. Her lips immediately pursed in a frown. As usual, she looked like shit. Her blond hair stuck out in about a thousand different directions—and she also had a small bruise on one cheek, thanks to a lucky shot by Ella.

Gaia blinked at her sour reflection. No, she was fooling herself. *Lucky* wasn't the word. Hardly. Ella hadn't had any lucky shots. Skill was what had enabled her to land that punch. If anything, Gaia had been fortunate to escape so relatively unscathed.

Whatever. She wouldn't concern herself with Ella right now. No, her stepmonster was locked away with George in their bedroom, doing God knows what. The poor guy. If he had any idea who Ella really was . . .

Mechanically Gaia went through the motions of primping. Hair brushed. Big clump of hair pulled off face and secured with a lone barrette. Nothing to be done about bruise on face. Baby powder? Didn't really hide it. All it did was give her a splotch of white on her already pale skin. She wiped it off. Wait. What about something for her lips? She dug through the vanity drawer under the sink and managed to scrounge up a lip gloss that Mary had bought for her months ago. It was a deep red shade, and Gaia wasn't entirely sure how to use it, but she stroked and used a fingertip to rub it around until her lips were covered.

Amazing. She almost looked like a normal teenager. Almost.

Quietly, or as quietly as she could in her steel-toed construction worker boots, Gaia slunk downstairs. She yanked open the foyer closet, grabbed her coat, and fled into the January night.

Don't think about Ella, she reminded herself as she headed toward her rendezvous. *Don't think about Sam. Don't think about anything.*

THERE WAS NOTHING LIKE A LITTLE

early evening lovemaking to put a sham marriage back on track.

Ella smiled at her husband, lying peacefully beside her under the rumpled covers, his chest slowly

The Wrong Woman

rising and falling in the easy rhythm of sleep. The afternoon couldn't have gone more perfectly. At these moments she almost felt . . . well, not exactly *tender* toward George—but at the very least sympathetic. The guy deserved to be happy every now and then. Especially since he had no idea that his life would soon be over. It was only fair. He wasn't a bad man, George Niven. He just happened to pick the wrong profession. To make the wrong friends. To marry the wrong woman . . .

"Honey?" Ella whispered. "Honey, are you awake?"

There was no response.

"George, dear?"

He managed a tired grunt.

She slid one smooth leg over his and ran a finger through his thinning gray hair. "Good," she whispered. "You need a rest. After all your hard work."

George blinked and opened his eyes, then shifted onto his side. "I'm sorry," he murmured drowsily. He tried to smile, but his eyelids closed again. "I don't know why I'm so tired."

It's probably the Seconal I slipped in your wine, Ella thought, grinning at him. But he probably assumed his exhaustion was a result of their recent . . . exertions. And that was what she wanted him to think.

"We should . . . we should talk to Gaia," he mumbled, yawning. "Find out why she skipped . . ." His voice trailed off. His mouth still hung open.

Ella nodded, scrutinizing his face for any signs of life. His breathing was once more soft and regular. "We'll talk to her soon, dear," she murmured. "I promise."

George began to snore. It was almost cute. And he would snore and snore until tomorrow morning. But she would wait beside him for a few more minutes— just to be sure he was truly out cold. It was always good form to err on the side of caution.

Then she could get up, wash his scent off of her, and head out. She had places to go. A person to see.

IN THE THIRTY SECONDS THAT IT

Kinky Contraption

took Heather to reach Ed's door from the time she buzzed his apartment, Ed figured his pulse had probably tripled. He didn't understand it. There was absolutely no reason to be nervous. None at all. Heather was here to watch a movie. Period. And she wasn't here to "watch a movie" (nudge, nudge; wink, wink)—the way they used to as a couple . . . which basically meant turning on the TV and ignoring what was on the screen for a few hours.

There was a very good chance that their kiss last Sunday was a onetime thing. There was a very good chance that it would never happen again. Which was fine with Ed. Really. Because he and Heather were friends first and foremost. So if Heather told him that there was no future between them, he'd be totally cool with it—

Stop lying to yourself, asshole.

"Ed?" Heather called, knocking again. She laughed. "Are you gonna let me in or what?"

"Coming, coming," he answered, trying in vain to shut up that annoying voice in his head. He unlatched the door and yanked it open, then wheeled himself back a few feet to give Heather some room.

"What's up, Shred?" she said with a big smile. "You know, it's not polite to keep a lady waiting."

Almost instantly Ed began to relax. When Heather was alone with him, she could always be counted on for a quick joke to ease the tension between them. He returned her smile, feeling a deep wave of affection for her. It wasn't just because she'd used his old skateboarding nickname, either. It was the whole way she *carried* herself, the way she was deliberately casual. Plus she wasn't all decked out like she usually was during the school week. Usually Heather strutted around looking like an MTV VJ. After all, she had an image to maintain. But by dressing down, it was almost as if she were silently acknowledging the fact that she never had to put on any kind of act with Ed.

In fact, the longer he gazed at her, the more she

resembled the Heather Ed used to know—her hair was down, loose, free. She wore a zippered, hooded sweat-shirt. Soft, faded jeans clung to her slim hips. Battered black loafers and green argyle socks completed her outfit.

Ed swallowed. The wave of affection began to turn to something else. Something a little more lustful.

Down, boy, he told himself.

But Heather didn't seem to notice the change in his eyes. She stepped inside and glanced around the apartment. Suddenly it occurred to him that she hadn't been here in more than two years—since a few weeks after his accident. A queasy sensation gripped his insides. Actually, the very last time she'd set foot in this apartment, she had come to break up with him.

So much for staying relaxed.

"It's nice to see that nothing's changed," she murmured, as if to herself. She looked down at him. "Where are your folks?"

Ed shrugged, striving to appear calm and cool. "Out until tomorrow. They went upstate to some bed-and-breakfast to spend the night." He shot her a rueful grin. "I guess they wanted to chill for a while after Victoria's engagement party fiasco."

Heather laughed. "Oh . . . that party wasn't a complete disaster," she said softly.

Their eyes locked for a moment. Ed's heartbeat quickened again. What had Heather meant by that enigmatic little remark? She wasn't being literal; that was for sure. The party *was* a disaster. Objectively. After all, Victoria had gotten wasted and humiliated herself, Ed's parents had clearly been miserable, and Blane's friends (Ed *still* couldn't believe that his sister was really marrying a guy named Blane) had trashed the grand ballroom of the Plaza Hotel in a drunken stupor. So Heather must be referring to something else: that being, of course, the little make-out session that she'd had with Ed in the storage room, hiding from the rest of the guests . . .

Heather's dark, perfectly arched eyebrows rose. "So we're alone, huh?" she asked in the same easygoing tone.

"Yeah," Ed said. His face was hot. He knew he was probably blushing. Great. Way to impress the ladies. He turned away from her and headed toward the living room. "You want something to drink?"

"No, thanks."

"So what do you want to watch?" he asked, parking himself beside the living-room couch. "Jackie Chan?" He stared at the blank TV screen, unable to keep from fidgeting. "Or maybe Jean-Claude Van Damme? I don't know if you remember, but the Fargo house is famous for action flicks." He listened to himself jabber away like an idiot, wondering when the hell he would be able to stop. "Or we could just channel surf—"

"Ed?"

He felt her hand on his shoulder. He looked up. She sat on the couch beside him, looking hesitant, innocent, vulnerable. Ed's heart clenched.

"Let's not watch TV," she said softly. "I really just want to talk. I mean, if I wanted to watch TV, I could have gone over to Megan's house or something, right?"

Numbly Ed nodded. He couldn't speak—not that he particularly wanted to. What was that old saying? *Better to keep your mouth shut and let somebody think you're an idiot than to open your mouth and remove all doubt.*

Without warning, Heather abruptly stood.

She kicked off her loafers, then passed through the living-room door and padded softly down the hall to his room—the first door on the left.

There was nothing to do but follow her. Feeling his heart pounding almost audibly, Ed pushed himself toward his ex-girlfriend. Blood rushed to every part of his body. There was something so surreal about the moment—as if he were acting out the choreography of a well-rehearsed, recurring dream. Here he was, alone in his apartment with Heather, like so many times before. . . .

She stopped a few feet inside his door. Her eyes flicked over the new elements of the room. Ed bit his lip. It had changed a lot since she'd last seen it. Instead of the former clutter (skateboards, clothing, sneakers), everything was spare, tidy, industrial. There was nothing on the floor to catch his wheels. His new desk was wide and had no chair since he just wheeled up to it. And his bed now had folded rails on each side. Over it was a hospital-type pulley system that he used to get himself onto the mattress.

Heather glanced up at the contraption, then turned and smirked over her shoulder.

Ed waited, his face a blank mask.

"Kinky," she murmured.

He exhaled, then found himself laughing. The girl was incredible. Truly incredible. Only Heather Gannis could pull off a line like that—sexy and offensive and teasing and intimate all at the same time.

Heather perched on the side of his bed. She looked so beautiful, so sexy . . . but once more, unsure of herself. The contrast made her infinitely more desirable. He could feel himself tumbling . . . falling down into a place where he wasn't sure he wanted to go. Unconsciously his hands tightened on his wheels.

"Ed," she whispered, looking into his eyes.

He nodded. "Yeah?" His voice was thick, clogged with emotion.

"I miss you," she blurted out. She lowered her head, staring down at her socks, hiding behind a curtain of hair.

"Oh," he said. Nice. Another brilliant response. He was Casanova on wheels. He blushed for what must have been the eighth time in the last twenty seconds.

"I can't get what happened at the hotel out of my head," she continued. "It's just, like, I don't know. Stuck there. And the weird thing about it is that . . . I don't know—it makes me happy. I think about it all the time. You know?" She drew in a sharp, quivering breath.

Ed gaped at her. His mind reeled. He couldn't believe it. It was as if he'd scripted those very lines for her. She was answering all his prayers, and she didn't even know it. Was it possible? Did she really want to go out with him again? Date him? Was she saying that she wanted to—

"Listen," Heather croaked.

His voice came out husky. "Yeah?"

"Could you do me a favor?" She looked up at him again and brushed her long, shiny brown hair over her shoulder. "I know this is going to sound really lame, like a teen movie or something, but could you please kiss me?"

Too bad he couldn't laugh at her joke. Because now his heart felt like it was going to burst right out of his chest. Given his luck, it probably would. He'd probably drop dead of a heart attack in the next ten seconds. At least it had been pitch black in the storage room of the hotel. At least he hadn't been able to *see* her. And she'd made the first move. But now it was up to him.

Ed wasn't even aware that his wheelchair was rolling slowly toward her. Heather's face just seemed to drift closer and closer until it filled his entire field of vision. She hesitated a moment, looking at him— as if giving him time to reject her, to push her away. But he couldn't. A fleeting thought of Gaia passed through his mind. It vanished the instant he smelled Heather's delicate perfume. *This isn't good*, that incessant, internal voice cried. *She's hurt you before. She ruined your life for over two years. . . .* But the words were lost in the swirl of desire and hope that rose up inside him.

He felt her breath, soft as a flower petal, on his cheek. His eyes closed.

This was the second time he had kissed Heather in the last week. It had been so long since he had felt desirable and attractive and . . . well, like an actual *guy*. Like a guy who was capable of having a girlfriend. It took only a second for him to surrender, and then her hands were gliding up his arms—and Ed almost felt himself again, almost whole.

43

TOM MOORE WAS NEARLY DONE.

Good thing, too. It was damn cold on the roof of the Nivens' brownstone. Even though his fingers were protected by specially crafted thermal gloves, they were losing

Something's Off

feeling. He shivered. A frigid wind had been blowing steadily for the past hour. His face and neck burned. But he had only two more connections to make. Then everything would be in place.

Deftly Tom pulled out his wire strippers and stripped the plastic coating off an inch of clear fiber-optic wire.

Perfect.

George didn't know about this receiver and transmitter. And he never would—at least not until Tom had proved his theory about George's so-called wife.

Ella was an agent.

For what or whom, Tom had no idea. But he would find out. And it was crucial that George be kept in the dark while Tom went about his work. There was no way George would agree to Ella's surveillance. There was no way George would ever suspect his darling, beautiful, urbane wife of something rotten. Love was blind. Or rather, love *made* you blind. Besides, so far all that Tom had on Ella were bits and pieces of circumstantial evidence: scraps of one-sided phone conversations, her mysterious trips to an apartment building on the Upper West Side— nothing concrete, no direct *proof*. But this new sound system would help with that. It was exquisitely powerful. It could pick up almost any noises within the brownstone, down to a whisper.

Once the wires were connected, Tom tapped them through the battery pack, then fixed the pack to the side of a crumbling black chimney—one of two at the front of the building. Then he pressed the wires down into the roof's tar and covered them with a malleable plastic sheath. Only a very close inspection (doubtful in this kind of weather, anyway) would reveal that these weren't cable TV connections.

Methodically Tom double-checked his work so far. He knew very well just how many operations had been ruined because someone had been too careless or arrogant to doubt their own skills. Self-doubt was what kept him alive. He measured the electrical flow with his voltmeter, then quickly gathered his tools. Strange, he reflected, that his daughter's room was only a few feet beneath him. He was doing all this for her—and she didn't even know it.

He felt a twinge of fear. He knew she wasn't home. At least when she was near George, she was safe. But Tom had seen his daughter leave only minutes ago, heading out into the city, to places unknown.

His jaw tightened. He wouldn't think about the danger his daughter faced. He wouldn't think about the fact that his best friend's wife might somehow be mixed up with Loki, his twisted twin brother—the very man who put Gaia's life at stake. Tom had a job to finish.

Slipping a minuscule earpiece into place, he listened carefully.

What the—

Almost instantly he was startled by the sound of some kind of animal in pain. He flinched. A few seconds later he heard it again . . . a groan that sent chills down his spine. What was going on in there? Frowning, Tom quickly spun dials, adjusting the quality and timbre. The sound of a woman humming under her breath floated into his ear. Suddenly the noises all snapped into focus, and Tom couldn't help but smile.

The sound he'd heard was George's snoring.

But then his smile faded. What was George doing asleep at seven forty-five on a Friday night? Of course, Tom well knew that agents often kept bizarre schedules, stealing catnaps whenever they could if they were forced to work around the clock. Very likely, George was just tired. Tom listened carefully and heard footsteps, receding slightly as they passed from one zone to another. Ella was heading downstairs.

She was probably going out.

Without hesitating, Tom pushed the earpiece more firmly into place and covered it with his dark knit cap. His eagle-sharp eyes raked the area for any telltale bits of wire sheathing or trash he'd left behind. Nothing. He was known for his clean work.

Below him, he heard a heavy door swing open— through his earpiece and also from down in the street. Noiselessly Tom crossed to the side of the building, slipped fine leather climbing gloves over the thin plastic ones he'd been wearing, and started to shimmy down the back of the brownstone.

His quarry was on the move. And he was going to follow her.

To: L
From: BFF
Date: January 19
File: 780808
Subject: ELJ
Last seen: Perry Street residence, 7:47 P.M.

Update: Subject observed leaving house and hail-
ing a taxi. Tail in place. Subject was not with
husband. Advise.

To: BFF
From: L
Date: January 19
File: 780808
Subject: ELJ

Directives: Continue to monitor activities.
Update as soon as she contacts/meets anyone.

Everything

he felt right

now was

melting

delicious

excitement

into one very

powerful

emotion.

Fear.

GAIA SHIFTED RESTLESSLY FROM foot to foot. Where was her uncle? Was she being stood up? Maybe this whole thing had been a practical joke. Maybe Oliver didn't want to see her after all. Maybe he'd been leading her on. It wouldn't be a huge surprise—not if Oliver was anything like Gaia's father. Oliver *looked* a lot like his brother, Tom. So why shouldn't he be a son of a bitch as well? He could be halfway to Tokyo by now. Or some other exotic place. Paris. Milan. Sydney . . .

Sweet Thing

Anywhere but here.

She glanced down at her watch, shivering. Icy clouds of breath exploded from her mouth in quick puffs. He was now officially a full fifteen minutes late. She'd give him until eight-twenty, and then she'd split, go get a slice of pizza or something. She didn't think she'd like Compagno's that much, anyway. It was too small, too crowded. The intimate little tables were all practically mushed against one another. It would be impossible to have any privacy in there. In fact, all of Little Italy was a little too crowded, too claustrophobic. The streets were narrower than in other parts of the city. It was like an ant farm for humans: dozens of little passageways, crawling with life. There were too many cars, too much action, too many bright lights and shouting voices—even in the dead of winter.

Gaia rubbed her hands together. Screw this. She would give Oliver one more minute. Then she was out of here. Maybe she'd go find Sam and kick his ass. She needed to do something—*anything*—so long as it would numb the sickness that was eating away at her gut. Anyway, why shouldn't she kick Sam's ass? She certainly was justified. He was a bastard. No, that was too kind. He was an unbelievably skanky weasel. At first she'd wanted to believe that his little tryst was mostly Ella's fault. But why? Sam was clearly so weak and pathetic that he couldn't keep his pants zipped—

"Hey, sweet thing."

Gaia's head jerked up. She hadn't even noticed, but some guy was standing next to her. Instantly she chastised herself for being so careless, so wrapped up in her own emotions. She'd been trained to detect a person's approach long before he or she was in striking distance. Not that she had anything to worry about in this guy's case. He was about fifty, just starting to gray at the temples—skinny and wimpy, dressed in a cheap blue suit.

She glared at him with a look of belligerent distrust.

Unfortunately, he didn't let that stop him.

"You look lonely, babe," he said in a smooth, oily voice.

"Looks can be deceiving," Gaia said frigidly. Her gaze grew harder, more threatening.

He didn't seem to notice, though. He laughed, showing lots of expensive teeth. "Oh, a smart mouth, huh?"

"It matches the rest of me," she replied. She scanned the streets, deliberately avoiding his eyes. Couldn't this idiot take a hint?

He laughed again. "You're too much. Listen—let me buy you a drink."

"I don't drink," Gaia snapped. "I'm underage. And even if I did, it wouldn't be with a scum like you." Maybe *that* would put the brakes on his libido. Forthright communication could scare off a lot of men. Particularly sleazebags.

"Oh, come on," the man said cajolingly. "You don't mean that. Am I so scary? Look at me." Again he flashed his teeth. They glinted in the pale light of the streetlamps.

Gaia leveled her gaze at him. "You're making a mistake," she warned simply. "If I were you, I'd beat it."

"Now you're talking to me, baby," he murmured, stepping closer. "I like that." He reached out and laid a hand on her coat sleeve.

Instinctively Gaia seized his hand and held it fast against her own arm.

His eyes widened. "Hey!"

With a flick of her wrist she twisted the man's arm—and he dropped to his knees. It was kind of funny, in a way. She'd used this exact same move against that idiot rapist in the park about a month ago. Very fitting.

"Let go!" he exclaimed angrily. "What the—"

Gaia exerted just the slightest amount of pressure on his wrist. He winced. His body sagged. Tears formed in his eyes. He was in serious pain right now. He breathed heavily, filling the air around them with boozy, frozen white vapor. Gaia smiled.

"I thought you wanted me to come with you," she said.

His face twisted with agony and rage. "Let me go, you bitch," he hissed. He tried to wriggle free but only ended up cringing.

"Bitch?" Gaia blinked. "I thought you said I was a sweet thing." Again she exerted pressure on his wrist. A little more and the bones would snap—just like that. She wouldn't mind hearing that satisfying crack, now that she thought about it.

The expression on the man's face was changing. He wasn't angry anymore. And Gaia knew why. Everything he felt right now was melting into one very powerful emotion.

Fear.

FROM BEHIND THE TINTED WINDOWS of his black Mercedes, Loki was able to drink in every element of this rapidly unfolding encounter. And he did so with glee.

A Profound Need

Gaia was a wonder. Truly a wonder. She'd subdued this ape in a matter of seconds—and she'd done so with an effortless skill and grace. And with a very admirable lack of remorse. Yes, there was something new in the way she handled herself. Something he hadn't seen yet. Something unforgiving. It was a trait he intended to cultivate.

He was certain that he could mold her in his image. After all, she was his blood. Genetically she was only one step removed from being his daughter; as twins, he and Tom shared identical DNA. She *should* be his daughter.

And she would have been if it hadn't been for certain unfortunate and mitigating factors.

But now it looked like she intended to break this man's arm—which would be an unnecessary complication. People were already starting to stare. Loki hopped out of the car and slammed the door behind him, then ran across the street. A few passersby turned their heads. He wasn't surprised. He knew he cut a dashing figure. He'd bought a new suit for the occasion: a sleek, black, pin-striped Armani. His patent leather shoes clicked on the pavement.

"Gaia!" he called.

She glanced up at him, but she didn't let go of the man. Her eyes narrowed.

"Are you all right?" Loki asked breathlessly, skidding to a stop beside her, his rugged face creased with feigned concern. "What's going on here?"

The man's terrified gaze flashed between Loki and Gaia.

"Help me," he croaked.

All of a sudden Gaia released him. The man crumpled to a heap on the ground. Gaia didn't even seem to notice. She simply stared back at her uncle—as if she didn't quite believe that he was actually here, standing in her presence. Loki fought back a smile. It was that same expression he'd seen on her face that day in the park . . . that look of surprise, and of longing, and of a profound need to make a connection.

Tonight would be their first real step in forging a relationship.

"Are you all right?" Loki repeated.

The man rolled across the sidewalk and scampered away from them, clutching his arm. Seconds later he staggered around a corner.

Gaia sighed, shaking her head. "I'm fine," she said. She lowered her eyes.

"What happened?" Loki asked.

She shrugged. "Some idiot tried to start some-thing," she mumbled. A troubled smile crossed her face. "I should warn you, that kind of thing happens a lot to me."

Loki chuckled, then reached out and gently patted her shoulder. He felt an almost electric tingle in his fingertips. This was truly a momentous occasion: the first time he'd ever touched his niece. Yes . . . tonight *was* an auspicious night.

She gazed up at him.

"Don't worry," he murmured. "That kind of thing won't happen to you anymore."

THE NEXT FIVE MINUTES PASSED IN

an utter haze. Gaia was barely aware of being ushered into Campagno's, of being seated by the hostess. . . . All she could do was stare at her uncle as he sat across from her at a cozy table for two. The restau-rant that had only moments ago seemed so cramped and uninviting had suddenly transformed: It was now *their* spot, *their* place—and the rest of

Pool of Sunshine

the world simply ceased to exist. She wasn't even exhausted from the fight (not that it had been *much* of a fight, of course). But she was too wound up, too confused. Adrenaline continued to course through her body. She gazed across the white tablecloth at him as a waitress poured water into their glasses.

"I am so sorry I'm late," Oliver said in a voice so like her father's, it made her shiver. There were some differences, though. His voice was more refined, a little more cultivated—as if he'd spent several years in a foreign country and picked up a hint of the local accent.

"I left the office in plenty of time but managed to get caught in traffic," he continued apologetically. "I should have known it was a bad idea to drive to Little Italy on a Friday night. If I hadn't been late, you might have avoided meeting that unpleasant man."

Gaia shrugged. "It's okay," she said. Then something occurred to her: He was coming from his office on a Friday? "Um, what exactly do you do?"

"I'm just a cog in a machine, I'm afraid," he answered with a self-deprecating laugh. He flashed a quick smile that reminded Gaia so much of her father, she almost felt dizzy. "I work in the research-and-development department for a . . . company." He seemed to linger over the last word. "Downtown. This is just their New York branch—their headquarters are in Germany."

"Oh," Gaia said. She felt a strange flicker in the pit of her stomach. She knew that he wasn't telling her the whole truth. "Company" was obviously a term that he used because he didn't want people to know what he did. And besides, if he was just a cog in a machine, then why all the secrecy about coming to find her? Why the allusions to danger, the cell phone number, the mystery? Even as these questions raced through her mind, she couldn't help but feel a delicious excitement, a sense of anticipation. Whatever secrets her uncle might have, she was certain he would let her in on them.

And then she would be part of something. Something *real*. At which point she could forget all about Sam and Ella and the rest of her miserable life . . .

"I'm hungry," Oliver announced. He grinned at her. "I hope you are, too."

Gaia nodded. Just at that moment a waitress appeared and handed them each a menu.

"*Alora, i piatti della casa sono i cozze, i carciofi parmigiana, e osso bucco,*" the waitress announced in Italian.

"*Momento,*" Oliver answered, holding up one hand. "*Vogliamo una bottiglie di vino rosso, del aqua minerale, e qualcosa di pane, per favore. Anche i cozze per tutte le due . . ."*

Gaia understood perfectly; she was fluent in Italian—he was ordering them red wine, water, bread, and mussels—but for some reason, she found she couldn't listen. In fact, for a moment she thought she might cry. Here she was, actually eating a meal with a real relative . . . in a quaint, expensive restaurant. All at once the place seemed to come alive. She soaked up every detail. The sound of laughter and clinking glasses filled her ears. Her nostrils flooded with the savory odors of basil, tomato sauce, and frying calamari. Her mouth started watering. Yes, she *was* hungry. But more important, she was warm; she was comfortable; she was content. She hadn't been to a place like this in years. Not since she lived with her parents.

Her uncle was bringing her back, though. Not just back to a familiar sort of place, either—but back to life. Yes. *Life.* Gaia blinked back tears. At this moment she didn't think she'd ever been happier. It was as if she were sitting in a pool of sunshine.

All I want is a little peace. That's not too much to ask, is it?

I mean, look at me right now. Seriously. I'm falling apart. The really scary thing is that it's only taken about four months for my mental state to completely collapse. At the beginning of the semester I was a pretty happy guy. Relatively normal. A sophomore at NYU. I had good grades; I had a hot girlfriend; I had a bunch of friends who liked me. Life was great.

Then I met a certain girl named Gaia Moore, and things started to unravel. Now I'm on the verge of failing out. All my friends are avoiding me—and when they aren't, it's usually because they're pissed off. Not that I blame them. I haven't been myself. I don't even know if I have a girlfriend anymore. No, instead I have some deranged stalker who happens to be Gaia Moore's foster mother, who

hounds me every freaking day
and night.

I guess it's pretty obvious
that Gaia Moore is the cause of
all my problems.

So why do I still think that
she's the only solution?

She took a second
to reflect on how
his sour expression
might change if
she suddenly **the**
pivoted, **last**
knocked him off
conversation
balance, and threw
him backward over a
neighboring table.

IT WAS AMAZING HOW GRACEFULLY

Ed shifted himself onto the bed. Watching him was like watching a gymnast. Not that Heather was particularly surprised. Ed had always been naturally coordinated,

Happiness Is a Warm Ed

a gifted athlete. Still, Heather couldn't help but stare at the taut, sinewy muscles in his arms. They weren't too big or bulging; they were just . . . perfect. He was no longer the boy she'd once dated. No. He was a *man*.

And she was a woman.

Right. She was having an epiphany. She was looking at the two of them in a whole new light. They'd both changed. They'd both matured. It was time to move forward. Together. He probably felt the same way.

She scooted back on the bed so he would have plenty of room next to her.

"What are you thinking?" Ed whispered, leaning back to make himself comfortable.

"That it was really nice to kiss you," she said simply. She lay beside him, nestling against his body, soaking in his warmth. She could hear his heart beating under his T-shirt.

He chuckled. "Funny. I was just thinking the same thing."

Heather smirked. "That it was really nice to kiss yourself?" she joked.

"I . . . I mean, no—you know," he stammered. "I—"

"I know what you mean," she murmured. She patted him gently on the chest and closed her eyes. Ed was so wonderfully insecure. Not in an annoying, self-pitying way—but in a perfectly charming way. How could any girl resist him?

Her eyes opened.

Actually, that was a good question. Maybe some girls *hadn't* resisted him. Had he been with anyone since the accident? Probably not. She would have found out. The rumor mill at their incestuous little school was surprisingly fast and accurate, largely due to Heather and her friends. But even the mere *thought* of him making out with someone else made her feel cold and shivery.

"What's the matter?" he asked.

"Nothing," she lied. She patted his chest again and closed her eyes. "You know, this may sound kind of weird, but you seem a lot bigger. You must weigh more."

He didn't say anything for a moment. He just stroked her hair. *Like old times*, she thought, too content to worry about thinking in cheesy clichés.

"Actually, I weigh almost ten pounds less," he finally answered. "My chest and arms are bigger, but I've lost a lot of leg muscle."

There was a catch in his voice—and it sent a pain through Heather's heart. For one brief instant she had a mental image of Ed two years ago, when he was Shred, king of the New York skateboarding scene. As if she were looking at a photo, she pictured the way his shaggy hair whipped through the wind, the way his oversized pants flapped as he jumped staircases. . . . It was best not to think about the past, though. She'd made a decision to sever herself from it. To prevent her lips from trembling, Heather leaned closer and kissed him again.

She felt his hesitation, his reserve. She couldn't blame him for that. All she could do was try to break through it . . . try to make him see how much he meant to her, how much she cared about him.

But Sam is my boyfriend.

No. Heather tried to block Sam's face out of her mind. It was surprisingly easy to do. Being with Ed felt so good, so right. Feeling this surge of strong emotions only showed Heather how weird and false her relationship with Sam was. She'd liked Sam Moon a lot; that was undeniable—but still, being his girlfriend had always felt so forced and uncomfortable, so unsatisfying. Sam was a great person. Heather knew that. But together they were no good, not anymore. She couldn't be herself around him. And she had to tell him how she felt. . . .

But right now all she felt capable of doing was kissing Ed, of sharing this moment. Sam was a billion miles away—part of another life, another world, another universe.

ONE OF SAM'S BEST QUALITIES WAS

Something So Cute

his predictability, Ella thought as she glanced at her watch. On Mondays, Wednesdays, and Fridays he staggered out of his dorm, sleepy and rumpled, no later than nine forty-five. He got home around four-thirty, then went out to eat no later than six-fifteen. On Tuesdays he was out by eight and not home until nine at night. On Thursday he was out also at eight but came home at eleven, then went out again at one and came home at three. On Fridays he was usually in the library most of the day. He went out at night.

And here it was, nine forty-five on Friday night . . . and here *he* was, in the Olive Tree Café on MacDougal Street. Luckily he wasn't meeting his supposed "girlfriend" (Ella was beginning to suspect that he'd just made her up) or freakish Gaia. He was with three boys—a bunch of regular college guys, also fairly cute—all of whom Ella had seen before.

Drawing her long, bloodred nails through her red hair, Ella crossed the street to the cafe. Her heels made a sharp tapping sound up the six worn steps. Once again the January night was bitter cold, but inside, the air was warm and thick with the smell of frying meat and beer.

Ella hesitated for a moment in the doorway. Sam was at a booth on the far side. She couldn't help feeling a twinge of excitement as she approached. It was strange: This boy—this peculiar, deluded *boy*—was the one pleasure she had in her life. Except for Loki, of course. But she wouldn't call Loki a pleasure. She would call him more of a . . . force. One that had consumed her for her entire adulthood.

But until Loki ceased his ridiculous obsession over Gaia, she needed her own distractions. Sam had served her well in that capacity on their one glorious night together—but he'd chosen to blow her off. Or he'd tried to, anyway. And that was unacceptable. He needed to take her seriously. No one had ever rejected Ella. This was *her* game, not his. The sooner he saw that, the easier it would be for both of them.

"So anyway," one of the guys was saying. "I've got this wicked—"

"Hello, Sam," she murmured, standing before them.

Conversation at the table came to a dead halt.

Four pairs of startled eyes glanced up at Ella. Three pairs were curious, appraising . . . even a little lecherous. Not Sam's, though. He actually looked shocked. Ella's lips pursed in a frown. No, he looked *horrified*. His skin was pale. What was his problem? In one instant Ella was ablaze with a burning anger—but her face remained inscrutable. Sam would learn his lesson. He didn't have a choice. He belonged to her now.

"Oh my God," Sam finally managed. His voice was little more than a gasp.

Ella reached out with one slim white finger, still bruised and sore from her encounter with Gaia, and trailed it along Sam's neck.

He flinched visibly and drew away. Ella's smile hardened.

"I've missed you," she said.

Three jaws dropped. Now, instead of staring at Ella, Sam's friends were gaping at *him*. He started shaking his head. His jaw twitched.

"What's the matter, sweetie?" Ella cooed. She drew back her fur jacket to rest one hand on her miniskirted hip. "Haven't you missed *me*?"

"Go away," he whispered. "Get out of here—"

"Aren't you going to introduce me to your friends?" Ella asked cheerily. Her gaze swept the table.

71

One of the boys smiled. Another one started choking on his french fries.

Abruptly Sam stood. The silverware on the table rattled as he pushed himself up and seized Ella roughly by the arm. "We need to talk," he growled without looking at her.

"Okay," Ella said calmly. She took a second to reflect on how his sour expression might change if she suddenly pivoted, knocked him off balance, and threw him backward over a neighboring table. But there was no point in creating a scene. Not yet, anyway.

Sam threw some bills down on the table and steered the two of them toward the door. It was too bad he insisted on leaving. Ella was just starting to warm up. Outside, the cold night air hit her like a slap in the face. She shoved her hands in her pockets as she clattered back down the steps to the sidewalk.

"What's the matter?" Ella asked, but this time her voice was colder, more strident. "You're not *ashamed* of me, are you? Come on, Sam. I'm—"

"Shut up!" he barked, jerking her around so that his face was now inches from her own. Ella grimaced. This close, in the glow of the streetlights, Sam didn't look quite as good as he had before. His eyes were wide, burning. His lips trembled. His hair and clothing were in complete disarray. If she didn't know better, she would say that he looked less like a college student and more like a junkie, a homeless teenager.

"I thought you said we needed to talk," Ella whispered, smirking.

Sam nodded, swallowing audibly. "Yeah. We do. But this is the last conversation we're ever going to have. *Ever.*"

Ella couldn't help but smile. There was just something so cute about Sam's attempt to be threatening.

THIS WAS THE SECOND TIME IN TWO

Shopaholic

weeks that Tom had seen Ella with the boy, Sam Moon. It was all the proof he needed that their meeting again was more than a coincidence. They were somehow involved together in whatever danger lay in store for Gaia.

A bitter bile rose in Tom's throat. To think that he'd once *trusted* this kid . . . that he had even gone so far as to contact Sam a few months ago in an effort to save Gaia's life. But what was Sam's role in this whole sordid business? Tom had no idea. Clearly, though, the boy was unhappy about something. He and Ella were arguing. From his vantage point in the shadows of a stoop across the street, Tom could see Sam stomping his feet and waving his hands.

Tom turned slightly so the broad-span microphone clipped to his collar could catch more of their conversation. So far, all the passersby and the street noise had totally obscured what Sam and Ella were saying.

He shook his head. He needed at least another day to plant more bugs on Ella's coats and jackets. She changed clothes too much. Not only was she cheating on George; she was robbing him blind with her shopping sprees. With Ella, every damn thing had to match some other damn thing. And she tossed out a lot of outfits after one use. Not even. Tom figured he would have to waste about twenty-five chips just second-guessing what she *felt* like wearing that day.

There was no point in getting angry over something that was out of his control, however. Right now he had to listen as best he could. But he could catch only the occasional word: "Forget . . . no . . . please . . . hassle . . . damn it . . . course . . . mean it . . ."

Rubbing his eyes tiredly, Tom pulled his wool cap farther down, over his ears. This was no good. He would have to get closer. Or he would just have to call it a night before he froze to death.

WITH ANY LUCK AT ALL, SAM WOULDN'T

Beyond Desperate

puke all over himself right now. Of all the screwed-up things in his life . . . He'd thought that cheating on Heather was bad enough. But to have this psycho, this *crazy* woman come after him, confronting him in front of his friends—it was too much. He was drawing the line. Tonight. It could go no further.

He took a deep breath and let it out slowly. "Let me make myself perfectly clear," he stated, finally letting go of Ella's fur coat. "*For the last time.* You're not going to follow me around anymore."

Ella shrugged. "If you returned my calls or my e-mails, I wouldn't *have* to follow you around," she said.

Incredible. The woman just didn't get it. Sam shook his head, suddenly oblivious to the cold, oblivious to the humiliation he'd just suffered back in the restaurant. . . . He was overcome by a strange sort of fear. No matter what he said, Ella chose to hear what she wanted to hear. He had a lunatic on his hands. A certifiable lunatic.

So maybe it was time to take a different approach—less anger, more understanding. He had to try *something*. He was beyond desperate.

"Look," he said, struggling to keep his voice calm and even. "I know this is my fault, okay? That night we were together . . . I mean, I was there just as much as you. And I'm sorry if you feel I was leading you on. But I was in a bad mental state. I was angry and depressed. And bombed—not that being drunk is an excuse. And you were there . . . and—and it just happened. But it can't go on. It can't happen again."

Ella blinked at him. "That's where you're wrong," she said.

God, help me. Sam felt like he was drowning. He didn't want to piss her off, though. Who knew what she could do?

"The thing is . . . ," Sam started to say, but he couldn't finish. He could only stare into those deranged green eyes, leering at him.

"I know you're angry for some reason," Ella said sweetly, coming closer. She raked her fingernails gently over his chest. A shudder shot down his spine. "But why does it have to be that way? You enjoyed it. You know you did. So did I. So why can't we continue to enjoy each other?"

Sam took a step back. He was starting to feel dizzy. She was too close. He could *smell* her—that dizzying, musky, perfumed odor.

"I—I can't," he stammered. "For one thing, I have a girlfriend. I feel bad about cheating on her, and I don't want to do it again—"

"Bullshit," Ella interrupted. She laughed, but there was a harsh undertone. In one second her eyes had changed from being soft and feminine to being cold, lifeless. "You don't care about your *girlfriend*. You hardly ever see her, Sam. That's not what's bothering you."

Sam stiffened. Ella was smart; he couldn't lie to her. "It's none of your business what's bothering me," he choked out.

"Oh, yes, it is," Ella whispered, closing the gap between them once again. "Because what's bothering you is *my* business, too. What's bothering you lives in *my* house."

All at once Sam's blood started seething. "Leave Gaia out of this," he hissed.

"Why should I?" Ella asked, raising her voice. She laughed again, without humor. "Don't you know how pathetic you're acting? Gaia doesn't *care* about you, Sam. You know that chess set you gave her for Christmas? *That* went in the trash December twenty-sixth. She *told* me to screen her calls because she doesn't want to talk to you. Don't you know anything?"

Sam was breathing fast, staring at Ella so hard that it seemed like he had tunnel vision. Everything else—the bright lights of MacDougal, the music coming from the used-record shop next door—it all faded away into an unintelligible blur. *She's lying,* he told himself quickly. *She's nuts, and she's lying. Don't believe her.*

Ella's face took on a look of pity and condescension. "Poor Sam," she mused.

"You're sick," Sam whispered, his voice trembling.

"Am I?" Ella asked. "Sam, *she* was the one who tried to beat me up when I told her the truth about us."

Sam gasped. *Told her the truth . . .*

At that moment the world went black. Sam couldn't answer her. His insides seemed to melt into acid. *Oh, shit. Oh, shit. Oh . . .* His worst nightmare had finally come true. Just as he knew it inevitably would. Gaia knew. About them. This was too much . . . too much information for him to begin to process, standing here on MacDougal Street. He needed to get the hell out of here. *Now.*

"Sam, what you need is a real woman," Ella said. "And I'm here for you . . ."

Ella kept talking, but Sam didn't hear the rest of it. He'd simply turned and started running—without any destination or direction, without even the slightest care of whether he lived or died. Because in a very real sense, his life was already over.

To: L
From: BFF
Date: January 19
File: 780808
Subject: ELJ
Last seen: MacDougal Street, 9:58 P.M.

Update: Subject observed arguing with Sam Moon.
The boy fled. Advise.

To: BFF
From: L
Date: January 19
File: 780808
Subject: ELJ

Directives: Tail the boy. Tail subject. If subject is not home by midnight, contact me.

A million scenarios of torture and retribution whirled **a** through his mind. He would **critical** make **moment** Ella pay for this. There was no turning back now.

"SORRY ABOUT THAT," OLIVER

apologized as he returned to the table, settling back in his seat across from Gaia. He smiled, his intense blue eyes seemingly boring into her own. "I'm afraid my workday

The Perfect Angel

never ends. When a beep or a call comes, I have to take it."

Gaia shrugged. "I don't mind," she said. It was true. Her uncle wasn't gone for longer than ten minutes. And during that entire time she wasn't once worried that he might not return. Not like some *other* members of her family.

"Would you like an after-dinner port?" he offered.

"Uh . . ." Gaia wasn't sure what to say. She didn't want to be rude, but on the other hand, she'd already had a glass of wine, and she was feeling a little woozy. Alcohol wasn't her favorite beverage. Not by a long shot. Still, sipping *vino rosso* with her uncle during dinner had made her feel so grown-up, so sophisticated. She hadn't even been carded, either. Maybe she should take advantage of the situation.

"Give it a try," he encouraged. "You might like it."

"Okay," she found herself answering. Just the sound of his voice made it almost impossible to say no to him.

He leaned back in his chair and nodded at the waitress. "You know, Europe is so much more sophisticated in this regard," he remarked.

"In what regard?" Gaia asked, feeling warm and drowsy. The table had long since been cleared. Every morsel she'd put in her mouth had been savory and satisfying. First she'd had bruschetta smeared with a black olive paste. Then her favorite: penne and calamari with black pepper and vodka sauce. Finally she'd been left to toy with a dense, heavy sliver of Italian cheesecake flavored with amaretto. . . .

"The drinking age," said Uncle Oliver as the waitress set two bulbous glasses down on the table, each filled with a tiny amount of a sweet-smelling amber liquid. He lifted one of the glasses to his nose, sniffed it, then took a sip.

He moves so fluidly, Gaia thought. With precision and control. Next to him, she felt ungainly and awkward. She would love to move as well as he did. Maybe she should start concentrating on it . . . trying to be that way. Trying to be more like him. He was so *classy,* too. He didn't even have to tell the waitress what he wanted. He only had to nod.

But what impressed her the most was his intellect. He was by far the most intelligent, experienced, and well-traveled man she'd ever met. Except for her father. And *he* didn't count.

"In Europe, parents supervise their children's

drinking," Oliver continued. "Children are offered a little wine mixed with water at a young age. That way they develop a sophisticated appreciation for one of the finer things in life. Alcohol is not a tantalizing forbidden fruit." He sneered. "In America the rules are so silly and arbitrary."

Gaia nodded, peering curiously at her own glass. Part of her wanted to wince. But the other part wanted to sip it, to really *enjoy* it . . . to "appreciate the finer things," to be a mirror image of this man. It was so odd, this feeling of wanting to measure up to someone's expectations. She glanced up, hesitating. "Have you been in Europe very much?"

He lifted his shoulders slightly. "I lived there for more than fifteen years. After Tom and I . . ." His voice drifted into silence, and his soft blue eyes met Gaia's again, seriously. "Well, after your father and I had our falling-out, I moved to Prague, then to Munich. Once I started working for my present employer, I moved around a lot. Copenhagen, Hamburg, Minsk, Strasbourg, Venice, Genoa."

There was that phrase again. *"Present employer."* He must have used it a dozen times this evening. Gaia felt an overwhelming temptation to ask him to be more specific, but she knew he must have had a good reason for not telling her. Maybe he was trying to protect her. Anyway, she didn't have to know the name of his company. She trusted him. Yes . . . she actually trusted him. God, why hadn't she called his number sooner?

"What's on your mind?" he asked softly.

She shook her head, then forced herself to take a sip of port. *Whoa.* It wasn't bitter at all, like the wine. It was syrupy sweet—deliciously so, with a pleasant smoky aftertaste. Maybe she *would* start drinking. A warm sensation filled her stomach, and she suddenly felt emboldened. "I was just wondering . . ." She bit her lip. "Why did you and my father have a falling-out?"

Uncle Oliver met her eyes. That was another reason she trusted him: He never looked away. Not like Sam, or Ella—or even George. "I guess you're old enough to know the truth," he murmured, a hint of sadness in his voice. "It was over your mother."

Gaia nearly dropped her glass. Her eyes bulged. *"What?"* she gasped. She'd had no idea that Oliver even *knew* her mother.

His gaze was unflinching. "Katia and I were engaged to be married," he stated.

Oh, my . . . Gaia slumped back in her chair. Her eyes were wide, unfocused. It was as if a giant eraser had swept out of the sky and completely blotted out her past. That happiness she'd thought she'd known with her mother and father, that brief period of bliss in their cozy house in

85

the Berkshires . . . all of it was suddenly tainted, poisoned by a secret none of them wanted Gaia to know. So her mother wasn't the perfect angel Gaia had always imagined her to be. Did any of this . . . Gaia swallowed, practically unable to complete the thought—did any of this have to do with her mother's death? And if so, how?

"We met while we were both in college," Oliver added quickly. "I fell in love instantly, of course. She was beautiful, intelligent, cultured. To me, it seemed as if my life had suddenly found meaning."

Gaia nodded, torn by a conflicting desire to run and hide and a desperate need to hear more. Her body pulsed with a wild energy. This was by far the closest she'd ever come to being afraid. It was as if she were driving by the scene of a horrible accident; she couldn't stop from staring. She didn't want to hear what Oliver had to say next. But at the same time she had no choice. . . .

"We became engaged," said Uncle Oliver. His voice flattened into a dull monotone. His eyes flickered down to the glass in his hand. He swished the liquid once. "I brought her home to meet my family. That was where she met Tom. On the day of our wedding I stood alone at the altar, waiting for a bride who never came. That was the day my brother secretly married the woman I loved. And that was the last time I saw either of them. Except . . ."

"Except for what?" Gaia croaked, her face pale.

"I saw them again the night your mother died. Unfortunately, when I arrived, she had already been murdered." He shot her a hard stare. "By whom, I don't know. All I know is that Tom disappeared after that, never to be seen again."

LOKI SIPPED HIS PORT, CAREFULLY

Final Mistake

studying his niece's face for any sign of what she might be feeling. This was a critical moment. He'd taken a risk—but it had been a calculated one, and the payoff was potentially huge. Anyway, all life was a series of risks. The trick was to place smart bets. Gaia already hated her father. And if she believed that Loki and Katia had once shared a love far deeper than Gaia's *real* parents had ever known, that Tom might have been responsible for Katia's death, and most important that Loki rightfully belonged in Gaia's life . . . well, then, Loki might just hold the key that would unlock Gaia's heart forever. Then she would be his. Finally his.

"I . . . I—I had no idea," Gaia stammered, staring down at the crumb-littered tablecloth.

"Of course not," Loki murmured. "Why would your mother and father tell you such a thing? It's too awful."

Gaia nodded absently. "You know . . . it makes sense," she whispered.

Yes. Loki felt a stirring in his chest. *Follow these feelings, Gaia,* he silently implored, staring down at her. *Trust your instincts.*

"It makes sense that my father never mentioned you to me," she finished.

Loki nodded gravely. "He had good reason."

Gaia shook her head and ran her hands through her hair. "I . . . I don't know what I'm even feeling right now." She laughed bitterly. "I mean, I thought *my* current family situation was screwed up."

An alarm instantly went off in Loki's brain. *Ella.* So Gaia's home life *was* falling apart, as he suspected. He knew now for certain that Ella's carelessness had destroyed Gaia's lone bastion of stability. And now the woman was out gallivanting around town, stalking that moronic boy whom Gaia prized so much. Loki fought back rage. Ella's little extracurricular activities were about to end. "What do you mean?" he demanded.

She glanced up at him, then paused.

"You know you can tell me anything, Gaia," he said, careful to keep the urgency out of his voice.

"That's why I'm here. That's why I gave you my number."

Gaia nodded. "I know. It's just . . . Okay, this is going to sound really weird. But I have this feeling that my foster mother isn't who she seems to be."

"What do you mean?" he pressed.

"We got into this fight," Gaia blurted out. The words exploded from her mouth and kept coming, as if a dam had been blown. "The thing is, Ella goes out of her way to pretend she's this trashy bimbo. But she's not. She's trained in martial arts. She's got a secret life. She nearly beat the shit out—oops." Gaia's face reddened. "I didn't mean to curse."

Loki waved his hand dismissively and leaned across the table. "Don't worry about it. I curse, too. So what you're saying is that Ella attacked you."

Gaia nodded. "Yeah. But luckily I'm a good fighter, too. Dad taught me a lot."

It took all of Loki's self-control to sit there and maintain his sympathetic expression. He'd never known a fury greater than the one he felt now. A million scenarios of torture and retribution whirled through his mind. He would make Ella pay for this. There was no turning back now. This was Ella's final mistake. He would do what he should have done long ago. She'd been assigned to *protect* Gaia. His eyes flashed to the slight bruise on Gaia's cheek. *My God.* At first he had attributed it to the scuffle he'd witnessed outside the restaurant. But now he knew better.

"Ella attacked you," Loki repeated, his voice slightly above a whisper. "Your legal guardian attacked you."

"Well, I mean, it wasn't out of the blue," Gaia muttered. She buried her face in her hands. "She just pisses me off so much. She's . . . disgusting, awful. I can't stand her. I hate living there. I hate it."

Loki found himself reaching for his niece, almost instinctively. He gently massaged her shoulder. "I'm so sorry, Gaia," he said, his voice thick with emotion. "I had no idea your living situation was so bad. If there's anything I could do . . ."

Gaia suddenly looked up. In that instant she looked so young—so beautiful, deceptively vulnerable, lost. A girl poised on the brink of womanhood. A bud ripe for the picking. This was the most delicate and cherished time of her life. There was no way Loki would allow Ella to destroy it. He knew he had to be the one—the only one—to share it with her.

"Actually," she said slowly, "maybe there is something you could do."

His heart leaped. "What?"

Her clear blue eyes met his, piercing him—right to the core of his soul. "Maybe I could come live with *you*," she said. "You're my uncle, after all."

Seduction Spot

POOR, IGNORANT BOY, ELLA REPEATED to herself over and over as she strode aimlessly through the frozen night. She was beginning to feel better, though. At first she'd been enraged that Sam had run off. Infuriated. But now . . . now she was glad that he knew that Gaia knew the truth about them. He deserved to know. It was only fair. Everything was out in the open. He was distraught—or at least he *thought* he was—but soon he would come back to her. He would see that a future without Ella meant no future at all. Once he realized that no other woman measured up to her, realized no one could satisfy him the way she did, he would come running.

In a way she even almost admired him for trying (however futilely) to maintain some semblance of honor. At least for a little while. She would give him a day or two to come to his senses, and then she would be ready to accept his apology. Yes. Everything would work itself out. And now that Gaia had gotten a taste of Ella's true capabilities . . . Well, there was no longer any need to worry about *her*.

Somebody jostled her on the sidewalk. She stopped, scowling—then all at once she paused. Where the hell *was* she, anyway?

She glanced up, checking out the street signs, soaking

in the crowded and brightly lit surroundings . . . and had to laugh. She'd walked east on Grand Street—east and east, all the way to Little Italy. She hadn't even realized it. At least she wasn't all *that* far from home. George was no doubt still snoring away. God, what a life. But the agony would last for just a little while longer. Just a little while . . .

Right now, however, she needed cigarettes. On the next corner was a deli—New York was so damn convenient, wasn't it? She hurried across the street, then paused on the opposite corner. Her eyes narrowed. Funny: She was right across the street from Compagno's, where she and Loki used to meet years ago. A sad nostalgia rushed over her as she stared at the restaurant, so cozy inside. Maybe her subconscious had driven her here for a taste of romance. She shivered. She hadn't experienced romance in far too long. She breathed deeply, filling the air with a white cloud. Loki had been so charming at first, so—

Her eyes instantly zeroed in on the unmistakable outline of a dark head, tucked away behind one of the curtained windows.

Loki. Yes. He was *here*. He was with someone, too. A woman. Ella started grinding her teeth. Instinctively she fished in her purse for a tiny pair of binoculars, then ducked into the shadow of a staircase. It was Loki, all right. Her part-time lover, full-time boss. So Ella wasn't the only one whom he tried to seduce at this place.

Men were so frighteningly typical, weren't they?

She focused the lens and trained the binoculars on his dining companion.

No. No. No ...

Her knuckles whitened as she gripped the cold black metal. This was impossible. Not her. Swallowing hard, Ella gazed at the two figures seated at the intimate table for two—*her* table, where *she* used to sit across from Loki ... marveling at his beauty, his strength, his power.

Gaia was there.

A bloodred haze filled Ella's brain. Without realizing it, she made a low, feral sound deep in her throat. So much for following Loki's orders. She had to take matters into her own hands. Fate, for whatever reason, had brought her here—and that cruel fate had showed her what needed to be done. Gaia's very hours were numbered now. The girl had to be wiped clean from existence. And soon.

"WHAT ARE YOU THINKING ABOUT?"

That Freak Gaia Moore

Heather murmured.

Ed wasn't sure how to reply. Here they were, lying on the bed ... just waiting to take the next step. The *inevitable* step.

The step they had taken together two years ago—back in a different lifetime, out by Heather's beach house in the Hamptons. Only now Ed knew that it could never be the same. And he wasn't thinking about the emotional side of it, either. No, *physically* it couldn't be the same.

"Ed?" she whispered, brushing her rumpled hair out of her face. She was leaning over him now, half covering his body with hers. Her face was flushed, sweaty.

"I was thinking how it was before the accident," he admitted quietly.

Heather took a deep breath, then sat up straight, disentangling herself from his embrace.

Oh, shit, he thought. Had he ruined any chance they might have had?

"This is good right now," she said finally.

"I know, I know," he said, hoping he didn't sound *too* eager to keep going. "It's just that it's hard for me." He swallowed, unsure of how clearly he wanted to express himself. "This whole thing. You know?"

She gazed down at him, her eyes softening. "Ever notice how people in really touchy situations always talk in really vague terms?"

"Yeah," he said thickly, trying to laugh. But he couldn't. He could feel his throat tightening, his insides churning. What the hell was his problem? Why was he screwing this up? He was in bed with a beautiful girl—the girl of his *dreams,* practically. How many sleepless nights had he spent fantasizing about this *exact* moment? Actually, he didn't want to go there. His desperation filled him with shame. "I just . . . don't want to let you down. And I don't want . . ." He couldn't finish.

"You don't want what?" she prodded gently, her face creased with concern.

He bit his lip, then turned away from her, staring at the wall. "I don't want you to let me down, either," he whispered.

"What do you mean?" she asked. Her voice took on a harder edge.

Ed forced himself to meet her gaze again. "I don't want this to be a onetime thing," he said. "I mean, I don't want you to ditch me the second you patch things up with Sam and—"

"This has nothing to *do* with Sam!" she snapped. All of a sudden her eyes started welling with tears. She jumped off the bed and snatched up her sweatshirt, pulling it over her body in quick, jerky motions.

"Heather, wait," Ed whispered, struggling to sit up straight. A terrible, wrenching sensation tore at his gut. He didn't want to hurt Heather—but at the same time he had to protect himself. He couldn't endure the pain of her rejection again.

It had nearly killed him the first time. She had to understand that. "I didn't mean—"

"Why did you have to bring up Sam?" she interrupted, glaring at him. She stood over the bed, her eyes smoldering.

Ed swallowed. "Maybe because you're still going out with him," he murmured.

Heather's eyes narrowed into slits. "That's low," she hissed. "I mean—that's really low. I didn't bring up the fact that you have a major crush on that freakazoid Gaia Moore, did I? No. Because I didn't want to spoil the moment."

The pain in Ed's stomach began to spread in waves throughout his entire body. He shook his head. "Heather, look, I—"

"Why don't you tell me what this is really about?" she barked. "Because I already know. The fact of the matter is that you don't think I'm good enough for you. That's it, isn't it? And you're just using Sam and your stupid accident as an excuse."

Something snapped inside Ed's brain. Pain instantly turned to anger. She had no right to accuse him of using his accident as an *excuse*. For anything. Ed might have done a lot of dishonest, sad, lowly, lame things—but he never, ever did that. *Never.*

"You don't know what the hell you're talking about," he spat.

"I don't?" she cried, her voice cracking. Tears began

flowing freely down her cheeks. "Then why are you being such an asshole?"

He shook his head again. "I'm not. I care about you, Heather. I . . ."

"You *care* about me? Oh, thanks! Thanks a million! Do I get fries with that?"

Oh, Jesus. There was that classic bitchy humor: the snappy comebacks he both loved and hated. In a way the little remark summed up the entire situation: Ed both loved and hated *her*, too. Everything about her. The way she was so beautiful. The way she acted. And he could never seem to sort out his feelings. He laughed miserably in spite of himself, but Heather was already tugging on her loafers and heading for the door. She stumbled as she tried to walk and get dressed at the same time.

"I'm glad you think this is funny," she growled.

"Heather, come on," he protested. "Don't go, all right? I'm sorry."

"Me too, Ed," she said. "Me too."

He flopped back down on the mattress. Well. So much for a little Friday night reunion. He should have just kept Heather confined to his fantasies. Reality was always a hell of a lot more complicated.

For the first time in my life, plans are coming together more quickly than I ever could have anticipated. Gaia has all but pledged herself to me. I had no idea she would reach out so quickly, with such abandon. Then again, I had no idea that Ella would fail so dramatically.

How could the woman be so foolish? Did she really think I wouldn't find out about her attack on my niece? Did she really think she could hide her depraved secrets from me?

But none of that matters now. I must keep my rage in check. I must act with decisiveness and detachment. Because soon my life will have no more room for rage. It will only have room for love.

The love of Gaia. My sweet Gaia.

His mind was blank. Maybe this was what prizefighters felt after they had gone ten rounds **a perfect ending** in the ring with the heavyweight champion.

STRANGE HOW NEW YORK CITY COULD change so fast. Only yesterday it had seemed like the most awful place in the world: a dingy, frozen wasteland overrun by perverts and psychopaths. But now it was as if Gaia were looking at it with a new pair of eyes.

Week of Weirdness

The grimy ugliness had transformed into cosmopolitan beauty; the unsavory characters now seemed to add to the limitless diversity. All right, yes ... the weather sucked, big time. But other than that, it was a great place to be. Perfect— if only Ella didn't live here as well. Or Sam, for that matter.

Only now it looked like there was a distinct possibility that Gaia wouldn't have to see *either* of them again.

She buried her head in the folds of her coat to protect herself from the bitter wind as she trudged east toward First Avenue. A part of her felt like skipping. She couldn't believe she had asked Uncle Oliver if she could come live with him. She hated asking anyone for anything. But the idea had just popped into her brain and from there had exited right out her mouth—and suddenly it was out there, *out there* in the open ... and he hadn't said no. He hadn't said no!

Okay, she knew she shouldn't get her hopes up. He hadn't said yes, either. Not exactly. He'd said that such a move would be complicated, but that they should have dinner again on Monday to discuss it further. Still, as far as Gaia was concerned, that was all the "yes" she needed. She was certain Oliver could handle whatever sticky legal matters would arise from getting the hell out of the Perry Street Penitentiary. Then her years of getting shuttled from one shitty foster home to another might finally be over.

She glanced down at her watch. It was nearly midnight, but she wasn't tired at all. Not in the least. Her brain was like a spinning wheel, imagining all sorts of future scenarios and conversations: "Oh, my uncle said he would take us . . . ," "My uncle gave me permission . . . ," "I'm meeting my uncle after school." It was a dream, yet it was real. A new life was about to begin. She just had to share the news with someone.

So she knew very well why her feet were leading her in this direction.

They were taking her straight to Ed Fargo's apartment.

She needed to talk to someone about this, and she knew that Ed was the only one in whom she could confide. It was time to end their ridiculous argument—or whatever it was. So Ed had spent some time with Heather. Big deal. Heather's sister was in the hospital. Heather *needed* a friend, a real friend—not any of the regular, shallow, narcissistic FOHs. And Gaia knew that Ed was far too decent a guy to deny somebody his companionship. No, if anything, this whole week of weirdness had been *Gaia's* fault. She'd been too caught up in her own problems to have any perspective. Which was typical. Gaia knew she could be a grade-A bitch.

But now it looked like all her problems had been solved.

Again she shook her head, reeling from it all. There were still so many things she needed to sort out. Was it really true that her father had engineered her mother's death? Was *that* what Oliver was trying to insinuate? Just the mere thought of it filled her with nausea. But Oliver spoke so cryptically; it was hard to determine what was real and what wasn't.

She picked up her pace. She was sure Ed could help her figure this out. Ed always came through. Always.

"COME ON, HEATHER." ED GROANED. "You don't have to do this. Really."

Heather refused to look at him as she yanked her coat out of the front hall closet. If she looked at him, she knew she would be overcome

104

by remorse. And she had to hold her ground. It was *his* fault this night had turned into a disaster. Not hers.

"So now you're giving me the silent treatment?" he teased.

She scowled at him, trying to ignore how cute he looked with his hair disheveled and shirt rumpled. "Shut up," she muttered.

"What do you want from me?" Ed demanded.

"I want you to get out of the past," Heather replied. "It's over. We're living in January, of this year, right here, right now. Remember? There's nothing either of us can do to change what happened."

Ed's face darkened. "You're right," he murmured. "We can't change it."

The accusing tone in his voice made her pause. She stared at him. His face was ashen.

"What?" he demanded bitterly.

"That's what this is all about," she said in a broken whisper. "You still blame me. You blame me for the accident. You've never forgiven me—"

Luckily, before she could start sobbing, something interrupted her. It was the sound of the buzzer.

She and Ed exchanged a quick, confused glance.

"I thought you said your parents weren't coming home," she mumbled.

"They *aren't*," Ed said, looking vaguely apprehensive. Not that she could blame him. Either the person buzzing was his mom or dad—or there was a complete psycho downstairs. Or a burglar. The options weren't exactly promising. Who else would show up uninvited at midnight in the dead of winter?

Ed rolled over to the buzzer and pressed the talk button. "Hello?" he answered.

"It's me, Ed. Can you let me up?"

Heather's jaw dropped.

Well. Damn. She recognized the voice. Instantly. Of course. There was no mistaking it. Funny: She'd been *right* about who was downstairs. It `was` a `complete psycho`. Gaia Moore certainly fit that category.

Ed's eyes flashed from the buzzer to Heather, then back again. She could see the blood draining from his cheeks. She couldn't help but laugh dismally. A `perfect ending to a perfect night, wasn't it`? Had Ed *planned* this? She wouldn't put it past him. He did have a screwed-up sense of humor that she'd never quite gotten.

"I—I wasn't expecting her," Ed stammered clumsily. He shook his head, his eyes wide. "Seriously, I have no idea—"

The buzzer rang again, loudly and insistently.

Heather rolled her eyes. No . . . Ed hadn't planned

this. He wasn't a liar, and besides, it was just too twisted—even for him. But of course, she knew he wouldn't turn Gaia away, either. He was too polite. She sniffed and marched to the door. "I'm out of here," she muttered, feeling very hollow. "This is getting way out of hand."

"Wait!" Ed cried. "We have to—"

"There's nothing more to say," she stated, opening the door. "Look . . . I know how I feel about you. And that isn't going to change. Nothing can change that: not your accident, not your being a total *asshole* tonight, not the fact that you blame me for what happened to you. Not even the fact that you insist on hanging out with that freak downstairs." Her voice broke, and she started to sob. She didn't even know what she was saying anymore; she had completely lost control. And she hated that feeling. She always needed to be *in* control. "But right now I have to get out of here. Right now I can't *stand* you."

With that, she slammed the door behind her. Tears streamed down her cheeks. Her entire body shook. She headed for the fire stairs. That way she wouldn't have to bump into Gaia on the way out. Judging from the state she was in, there was a very good chance she might just kill Gaia Moore if she saw her tonight.

ELLA PUFFED FURIOUSLY ON THE

cigarette—her third in twenty minutes. The hot smoke warmed her insides. Her strides were swift, deliberate. People stepped aside for her, as well they should have. She was in no mood to be polite tonight. Fortunately she would be home soon. The brownstone was only a few more blocks down West Fourth Street. What she really needed right now was a drink. Yes . . . a soothing, numbing drink to blot out what she had seen back on Mulberry Street.

The Test

No matter how hard she tried to forget, or rationalize, or shrug off Loki's dinner with Gaia at Compagno's, her mind kept coming back to the same question: Why hadn't he *told* her that he would be meeting his niece there? What motive could he possibly have? The answer, too, wouldn't go away. And it chilled her with a far greater intensity than the blustery winter night.

Loki was cutting Ella out of his life.

He had a new agenda now, one that didn't involve her in any way. She drew deeply on the cigarette, shaking her head as she rounded the corner onto Perry Street. Once an operative was out of Loki's sphere, then it inevitably followed that he or she would be out of the realm of the living. Ella knew she'd let him down a few times, but his recent behavior with her had been so tender. So forgiving. She swallowed. It had all been an act, obviously. And it would take more than a couple of glasses of wine to help her deal with what lay in store for her.

She stopped short suddenly, debating whether or not to buy a bottle of liquor for herself. Yes. She needed something—*anything*.

She turned and to her utter shock found herself face-to-face with a dark figure. The cigarette dropped from her mouth, tumbling end over end to the side-walk.

"Loki," she whispered.

He nodded almost imperceptibly, his cold blue eyes like dead stones in the night.

Immediately she felt a flutter of hope. He must have seen her outside the restaurant. Of course—he'd seen her and followed her home, abandoning Gaia. *Abandoning her for me*, Ella thought. So she *wasn't* in mortal danger. Not yet, anyway. A shaky sigh passed her lips. She reached out to him, running her fingers across his coat sleeve.

"I'm glad you followed me," she murmured.

He stepped back, out of arm's length. "I . . . I have to go," he mumbled. His voice sounded strangely high-pitched. He whirled and ran back toward West Fourth Street, melting into the shadows of the park.

Ella gaped after him. What had *that* been all

about? What was he trying to do? Did he want her to follow him? She frowned. He was clearly playing some kind of game with her, subjecting her to some kind of test. So maybe he *didn't* want her to follow him. That would be the obvious thing to do. The *weak* thing. Loki prized strength above everything else. If she simply ignored him, if she simply continued on her way, she would be proving to him that she was self-reliant. She would earn his respect again.

That was what he wanted, wasn't it?

Shaking her head, she turned back to the brownstone. A shudder ran down the length of her body. She didn't know whether to feel relieved or unnerved. One thing was for certain, though. She needed that drink now more than ever.

ED HAD NO IDEA WHAT HE WAS

feeling as he waited for Gaia to come upstairs. None at all. He was perfectly numb. His mind was blank. Maybe this was what prizefighters felt after they had gone ten rounds in the ring with the heavyweight champion.

110

Or lobotomy patients after their operations. Anyone who had suffered major head trauma. He felt beyond drained. Beyond *anything*. Just . . . zilch.

Normally he would have been thrilled that Gaia had dropped in on him by surprise at midnight. Normally he would have been thrilled that Heather had all but invited herself over and thrown herself at him. Normally, normally, normally—

There was a loud knock on the door.

"It's open," he mumbled.

Gaia quickly stepped inside, then frowned as she looked Ed up and down. He didn't even care that his shirt was untucked or his fly was unzipped. Caring took too much energy.

"Did I come at a bad time?" she asked tentatively.

Ed grinned and ran a hand through his tousled dark brown hair. "Something like that."

Gaia frowned.

"Heather was just here," he stated. Surprisingly, it was a relief to just come out and admit the truth. He was too exhausted to try to put up a front. Besides, Gaia always ended up seeing through his lies, anyway.

Remarkably, she didn't even seem bothered. She peered at him closely. "Ed, are you all right?"

"Me?" He jerked slightly. The question caught him off guard. "Uh . . . yeah."

Gaia's face softened. She smirked. Then her brow grew furrowed. "Do you know that I can see your underwear right now?"

Ed nodded. His shoulders sagged. He reached down and yanked up the fly on his jeans, then turned and rolled toward the living room. Gaia followed softly behind him.

"I interrupted something between you guys, didn't I?" she asked.

"Not really," he answered. In a way, that was the truth. Whatever had been going on between them had stopped long before Gaia had showed up.

"Come on, Ed." She quickly stepped in front of his wheelchair and leaned over him, resting her arms on the rails. "You can talk to me about this."

Ed blinked at her. Now *this* was a weird turn of events. He was always encouraging *her* to open up—and the one time the roles were actually reversed, he was refusing. An event like this was about as commonplace as a total eclipse of the sun.

"Um . . . aren't we supposed to be in a fight right now?" he joked.

Gaia smiled. "That's why I'm here. To end it." Her grip tightened on the sides of his chair. "But I'm not letting you move until you tell me what's wrong."

He swallowed, his gaze roving over her face, but then he bowed his head. He just couldn't do it.

He couldn't bring himself to relive the night again.

"Well, then just answer me this," Gaia said wryly. "Is everyone on earth getting some except me?"

That made him crack a tiny smile. "You had your chance," he whispered, unsure of whether he was kidding around or not.

"I know," she said, playing along. "And I've kicked myself a thousand times. I guess it wasn't meant to be. In the meantime . . . are you in love with Heather?"

Ed flinched. "No," he snapped, frowning. He shook his head. "No. I can't stand her. I hate her."

But Gaia just kept grinning. "Ed," she said as kindly as he'd ever heard her, "we have to work on your lying skills."

Ed Fargo. The joker. The guy
who has an I Brake for
Leprechauns sticker on the back
of his wheelchair. The guy (one
of the few) who truly appreciates
Krispy Kreme doughnuts. The guy
who has always been just plain,
goofy Ed.

I guess what I'm trying to say
is that he's never been an
option . . . romantically, that
is. But when I walked into his
apartment and saw the state he
was in, with his shirt out and
his hair so messy, I have to
tell you—objectively, he's good-
looking. Really good-looking.
And I know that doesn't make any
sense, but people always look
their best to me when they're
sloppy.

But for some reason, I've
never even considered that somebody might think of Ed in those
terms. Especially Heather Gannis.
But I have to admit, there seems
to be some actual emotion here on
Ed's part.

So where does that leave me? There's Heather and Sam, Sam and Ella (I don't want to think about that), and now Ed and Heather. . . . A pattern seems to be forming. Lots and lots of hookups are going on, and I'm the only one who isn't involved.

These are my teenage years, and while I don't want to go around being a total slut, it would be great if *someone* would show some interest in *me* once in a while.

But that's not the point. The point is, I've made up with Ed. I've even accepted the fact that he likes Heather. I've even (and this is the really big one) accepted the fact that Sam is a total asshole and that I never want to see him again. I'm moving on. And Ed is the only one I'm taking with me. I've got a new mission in life: to become part of a family again.

So in some ways, I guess nothing has really changed.

Sam grabbed Mike's hand to check for a pulse. It was only then **place** that he saw the **of** hypodermic syringe **worship** still sticking out of Mike's left forearm.

SATURDAY MORNINGS ALWAYS MADE
Tom think of Katia. She had
been old-fashioned in many
respects, and it had only contributed to her sense of mystery.

Amateur

Even after they had settled in America—traveling in
sophisticated circles, privy to top secret governmental
information—still, on Saturday mornings Katia
always tried to go to synagogue.

When they were in New York, she went to a small,
conservative temple on St. Marks Place. Several times,
in fact, they had taken Gaia to Shabbat services there . . .
all of which made this moment all the more disturbing.

Here he was, on a Saturday morning in New York,
and instead of watching Katia prepare herself for
religious observance, Tom was trailing Ella Niven,
watching as she approached the Little Village Church
on Astor Place for a nondenominational ten o'clock
service.

There was no way she was going to worship—he
could tell *that* from the way she was dressed. She was
wrapped up in a thick brown leather car coat,
trimmed with fake leopard fur. Her matching spike-
heeled leather ankle boots made a rapid *rat-a-tat-tat*
on the church steps like an automatic weapon. Not
exactly the garb of a pious devotee. She had to be
meeting someone.

Loki, probably.

Tom shuddered once. The memory of last night's bizarre encounter still clung to him like a layer of some kind of vile slime. She'd actually believed that *he* was Loki. Of course, that was precisely what he'd wanted her to believe. He was still furious that he'd allowed himself to get caught tailing her—but he'd reacted to the situation in a split second, slipping into a role . . . a role he knew better than any other. His years of training had paid off handsomely in that moment. Yet he felt so many conflicting emotions: shock at the obvious sexual nature of Ella's relationship with his twin, rage at her betrayal of George—but most of all, horror. Horror at the fact that Loki had been so close to Gaia for so long.

None of that mattered at the moment, however. Tom couldn't allow his feelings to cloud his judgment or impede the task at hand. He hadn't last night. He was a professional. He had work to do.

He picked up his pace and followed Ella through the thick double doors.

It took him a moment to get used to the slightly dimmer light. The air was warm and stuffy, and despite the vases of fresh flowers, still, the church had a sad air of neglect. Rich organ music filled the room. There were only about eight people in the pews. But that made it easy to see the dark figure disappearing down a side aisle toward the emergency exit door.

Tom sped after her, ignoring the few startled looks he received. Ella had passed through the emergency exit soundlessly—but as soon as Tom opened it, a huge, clanging alarm sounded.

He froze for a moment, stunned. *Damn!*

Now Ella knew that she was being tailed. He shut the door firmly behind him and found himself in a dark, narrow alley that obviously saw daylight only at noon in the middle of summer. Luckily he caught a glimpse of her disappearing behind a brick wall at the end of the passageway. Running as silently as possible, Tom pursued her.

He flew down the alley, dodging garbage cans, startled rats, dank puddles lined with scum and mold. At its end he turned right, almost bouncing off the wall to make the turn fast. *There!* Once more he caught a quick glimpse of her. His nerves immediately started to tingle. That was too neat, just a bit too easy, wasn't it? Maybe she was setting a trap. An experienced agent would have lost him by now . . . and there was no longer any doubt in his mind that Ella was an experienced agent.

He shot out the entrance to the alley—and almost got run over by a truck.

"Whoa!" he gasped.

He flung himself backward at the last second, almost tumbling over a bench. With his breath coming fast and pulse racing, he scanned the street. Ella was nowhere in sight. Of course. She'd drawn him straight into a busy thoroughfare in hopes that he would get flattened. He scowled. She'd toyed with him. She'd managed to lose him as if he were an amateur.

Tom cursed himself for being a fool. Although—wait a minute. He wasn't too far from NYU. He could go check on Sam Moon.

Who knew . . . he might even run into Ella there.

The Big "If"

ANOTHER SATURDAY MORNING, ANOTHER sleepless night.

Sam sat on his unmade bed, gazing over the mess that smothered his entire room. It was amazing how one's living conditions worsened in perfect proportion to one's sanity. He sniffed once, then grimaced. He could smell the stink in here. Not a good sign. Saturdays were a lot different now, weren't they? A few months ago he would wake up after a long sleep and think: *All right! Saturday!* No classes, no labs. Just regular homework duties, hanging out, maybe a football game later . . . and of course, a routine phone call to Heather.

A twinge of guilt shot through him.

Heather ...

All of a sudden he had a flash of the whole ugly scene with Ella last night. He went cold and clammy. He rubbed his hands over his face. It was all his fault. If he hadn't been shit faced the night he'd met her, if he hadn't just found out about Heather and Charlie Salita, *if, if, if* ... `if he wasn't a spineless jerk with the morals of an alley cat, then he wouldn't be in this mess.` It was a big "if." And now Gaia knew the truth, too. Which meant that he was truly and royally screwed with the one person he felt might be his soul mate.

But maybe Ella was just making that up. Maybe she'd just been yanking his chain. That seemed to be a specialty of hers.

And maybe he was just a confused, messed-up kid going through a bad time.

Yeah, right. He was a jerk. But if he could just have a fresh start, a chance to clear everything up, a chance to put things right ... then everything would be okay.

Sam glanced at the window. Morning light was filtering in through the sagging and bent venetian blinds. He needed a plan. Only, it was hard to prioritize. Grades? They wouldn't be hard to fix. He could study like a madman, not miss a single lecture, take great notes. Yes. He felt a surge of confidence—but that could have just been due to sleep deprivation.

No, no . . . he could do this. He would fix one thing at a time.

What was next? Heather. Of course. He had to break up with her. But in a nice way. Let her down easy. Let her know it wasn't her; it was him. That she deserved someone better. Good. That was a good plan. As soon as he got up and took a shower, he would call her and ask to get together soon. She wouldn't even be that upset. After all, the last time he'd seen her, she'd run away from him. And why not? He'd shown up at her school, looking for Gaia and acting like a madman. Heather would *thank* him for letting her off the hook.

Okay. Heather problem taken care of.

That left Gaia. The tricky part.

Suddenly Sam felt like it was time to go take a cold shower. He needed to be awake, alert, to shake off his sleeplessness. He stood up and lurched toward his door. He'd seen Gaia—was it just yesterday? The day before? But nothing was ever normal between them. It never had been. They'd had nothing but one weird misunderstanding and messed-up communication after another ever since they had met.

He had to get it all straight. He had to see what was going on in her head, how she felt about him. Most important, he had to tell her how he felt about her. And he had to warn her that she was living with a psychotic maniac.

That last part might be a little tricky.

But he could do it. He had to. Somehow he just knew they were supposed to be together, that everything in his life up until now was leading him to her. They were like pieces on a chessboard—and the chessboard was the entire city of New York—and while each move put them in greater peril, the moves also brought them closer. Yes. It was destiny. Somehow he would convince her to give him a chance. And then she could explain exactly what the hell she had been doing, ignoring all his e-mails, his phone calls, and his chess set.

Yawning and stretching, Sam headed out into the small, dingy common area he shared with his two suite mates. He snickered as he saw Mike Suarez slumped against the ragged foam couch, mouth open. Now *here* was somebody who was enjoying the college life. Evil stalkers and kidnappings played no part in Mike's NYU experience. Nope. He just went out and got so wasted that he couldn't even make it to bed. Good for him . . .

But then Sam paused for a moment.

Mike actually looked *really* bad. Jesus. How much had he drunk last night? Sam hadn't even heard him come in. Sam crouched down beside the couch. His pulse immediately quickened. Mike's eyes were open a tiny slit. There was foam flecking the corner of his mouth. His skin was cold and gray. *Shit*. Sam grabbed Mike's hand to check for a pulse.

It was only then that he saw the hypodermic syringe still sticking out of Mike's left forearm.

THE MOMENT BEFORE WALKING INTO

Put on the Cheerful Face

the hospital room was always the worst part of the visit.

Once Heather was inside, sitting beside her sister and chatting away, she was fine. She was comfortable. But it was just that initial moment— the moment of opening the door and seeing Phoebe in bed, so skinny and pale, almost *translucent*, hooked up to a million tubes and wires ...

Whatever. *Thinking* about it wouldn't make it any easier.

Drawing in her breath, Heather forced herself to turn the knob.

"Hey, Feeb," she said breezily, strolling across the linoleum floor, deliberately avoiding looking at the bed. She squinted in the morning sunlight as she placed a small potted African violet on the windowsill. "I saw this little plant in the gift shop. I couldn't resist it. See the tiny pink flowers?"

From under her covers, Phoebe looked over at the plant and nodded, managing a faint smile. "It's pretty," she murmured. Her voice was hoarse, raspy.

Heather took off her coat and dropped her purse on the ugly vinyl armchair, then smirked. "Can you believe I actually bought a plant?" she asked.

Phoebe laughed. Almost instantly Heather felt better. The laugh sounded strong, almost like the old Phoebe. Was she recovering? Would she get out of this awful place sometime soon? Maybe if she did, Heather would feel ready to go back to her old life. With her old friends. She suddenly realized she hadn't talked to anyone but her parents, Phoebe, and Ed in the last week. It was scary. Of course, she didn't want people to feel pity for her just because she had a sister in the hospital. Pity led to avoidance—which led to loss. But still, she couldn't help but wonder, why hadn't her friends been calling her? Had she *already* lost them?

No. Of course not. Her friends were still there for her. She just needed to reestablish the connection. Anyway, a few of them *had* left messages, but she just didn't want to deal with them. Mostly they'd wanted to know about Sam. And this was neither the time nor the place to get hung up about it. She stood over the bed and smiled down at Phoebe.

"If the plant gets enough sun, it'll bloom all year," she said. "That's what they told me."

"Cool," said Phoebe. "It'll be nice to look at." She raised her blue eyes. At least *those* had some life in them—even though they were ringed by dark circles, even though they seemed so huge now in her gaunt, almost skeletal face. "So how's it going?"

"Oh, fine," Heather said automatically. She pushed her long, dark hair over her shoulders. "It's chilly out there. I'm sick of this weather. Remember that year Mom and Dad took us to Disney World, and it was like eighty degrees in the middle of winter—"

"Heather?" Phoebe interrupted.

Heather blinked. "Yeah?"

"You look like shit. What's going on?"

For a moment Heather was startled. A little annoyed, in fact. But strangely, she was encouraged at the same time. If Phoebe was alert enough to notice that Heather was having a bad hair day, then Phoebe was definitely on the mend.

"I'm fine," Heather lied. "What do you mean?"

Phoebe pursed her lips. "Heather, I'm sick, not stupid. You're talking about the weather. You *never* talk about the weather."

Heather laughed. But then, for some unfathomable

reason, her laughter abruptly stopped. All of a sudden she started crying. What the hell was her problem? She was never this out of control. But the more she thought about it, the harder she cried. This was just great. She was having a mental breakdown in front of the sister who'd already suffered a mental breakdown of her own. For God's sake, she was here to put on a cheerful face. With a gasp of indrawn breath, she collapsed into the chair next to her purse.

"It's Ed," she finally managed.

Phoebe's face creased with worry. She struggled to prop herself up against the pillows. "What about him? Did something happen?"

"No, no." Heather shook her head and sniffed, shifting uncomfortably. She rubbed her face with the sleeve of her sweatshirt. "It's just, uh . . . we kind of hooked up last night."

Phoebe's mouth fell open. *"Really?"* she cried. The raspiness in her voice was gone. A smile spread across her face. "What happened? Tell me everything."

A last tired laugh escaped Heather's lips. It was amazing how a little sordid gossip could revitalize a sick person. Oh, well. At least Heather's misery was serving *some* positive purpose. They should just get rid of all the IVs in this place and send people around to spread rumors. Then everyone would get better a hell of a lot quicker.

"There's nothing much to tell," Heather finally admitted. "I mean, I went over to his place, and it just kind of happened. It didn't go very far, though."

Phoebe peered at her closely. "You know what I'm going to ask next, don't you?"

"What?" Heather groaned. "Did we do the nasty?"

"No!" Phoebe laughed, then tossed one of her pillows at her sister. Unfortunately she was still so weak that it fell to the floor at Heather's feet. "What about *Sam?*"

Oh. Right. Heather hadn't even thought of that. Which pretty much summed up the situation. She shrugged. "I don't know what's going on with Sam. All I know is that I'm not happy with him. It's been building up for a while. And when I went to Ed's sister's engagement party, I suddenly realized that I still had feelings for Ed." She wiped her face again. "I still want to be with him, I guess."

"Wow," Phoebe murmured.

One of the machines beeped softly. Phoebe glanced up. Her IV drip was empty.

"What is that?" Heather asked, mildly alarmed.

Phoebe frowned wryly. "Nothing. Glucose. They're trying to fatten me up. Like a Thanksgiving turkey."

Too bad it isn't working, Heather thought, but she kept her mouth shut. There was no quick fix to this situation. Phoebe's recovery was going to take a long, long time.

"So tell me more about Ed," Phoebe prompted.

Heather hesitated. "I really didn't mean to dump this on you," she said.

"Please," Phoebe groaned. "It's not like I'm busy or anything. Besides, your problems are much more interesting than mine. Spill it."

"Well." Heather slumped back in her chair. "I don't know. I'm just really confused. I mean Ed is so excellent, so adorable . . . and a total asshole."

Phoebe chuckled softly. "Two out of three isn't bad."

Heather just moaned.

"So are you going to break up with Sam?" Phoebe asked.

"Yeah. Even if things with Ed don't work out, I know that Sam and I are through."

"Great! Maybe I can have him."

Heather jerked her head, scowling.

"Just kidding," Phoebe wheezed. She laughed weakly, then started coughing.

All at once Heather's face softened. She started laughing and crying at the same time again. Jesus. What would she have done if Phoebe had died? They'd had so many ups and downs over the years, but recently Heather felt like they'd made a breakthrough in their relationship. They'd moved past the bickering-sibling stage. They were becoming *friends*.

And then Phoebe started wasting away before Heather's eyes.

"I hope you work it out," Phoebe said at last.

Heather nodded. "Me too. But I don't know if that's possible. I don't know if *anything's* possible."

MIKE OD'D. MIKE MAY BE DEAD.

Unanswered Question

Mike...

Sam jumped to his feet. "Brendan!" he yelled. "Brendan! Get out here!"

But there was no answer. Sam began to panic. They had one other suite mate, but it looked like he wasn't home. Sam raced to Brendan's room and pounded on the door. Nope. Sam was on his own.

Okay, okay. He couldn't lose control. He had to think straight. Each passing second further endangered Mike's life. He scrambled back to his own room, nearly falling on his face—then lunged for the phone across the ever present pile of books and filthy laundry. With his fingers shaking, he dialed 911.

"Emergency," a female voice answered.

"My friend OD'd," Sam whispered. His voice was quavering so much that the words were barely intelligible. "I need help."

131

"Calm down, sir," said the emergency operator. "Tell me where you are."

"In the NYU dorm on Eleventh and Fifth. Fourth floor. Rooms four through seven." Sam craned his neck, peering back into the common room. He was starting to hyperventilate. "Hurry! I think he's . . ." He couldn't bring himself to say it.

"We'll be right there," she said.

Sam slammed the phone back on the hook and raced back to Mike. After carefully removing the needle, he stretched his friend out on the ancient, beer-stained carpet. Mike's breath was so faint and shallow that Sam could hardly detect it. He put two fingers on Mike's neck. Then he started rubbing and patting Mike's hands firmly.

"Mike, man, you screwed up," he found himself muttering. "What the hell were you thinking? When did you—"

All of a sudden Mike's eyes fluttered, then rolled back in his head. His back arched slightly, then he relaxed. He quit breathing. His pulse was gone.

No. No. No . . .

Without thinking, Sam jumped up and ran to the suite door, flinging it open. "Help!" he shouted. "Somebody help!"

Again no answer. But it didn't matter. Sam

knew CPR. And now he had to use it. He was premed, after all; he'd better get used to crises like this. His mind seemed to shut off as he darted back to Mike and went to work. Pinch nose, breathe out, count, breathe in . . . Where was that frigging ambulance? Sam breathed into Mike's mouth again, firmly and steadily, then sat up and compressed Mike's chest four times: one, two, three, four. Then another breath. Then chest compression.

"Come on, Mike," Sam grunted, desperately fighting back panic. "Start breathing!"

One, two, three, four . . .

Mike gasped faintly. Sam repeated the technique. Yes . . . Mike had a pulse. Sam found himself grinning maniacally. He was doing this! He clutched Mike's wrist, unaware how much time was passing. All he knew was that the color of his friend's face was changing from waxy gray to a pale, sickly yellow.

There were pounding footsteps in the hall. Sam whirled around. Two paramedics burst through the door with a portable stretcher.

"His heart stopped," Sam said faintly. "I did CPR. . . ."

"Good for you, kid," one of the paramedics said.

Sam stood up and stepped aside so that the EMT unit could do their job. His knees were wobbly. He couldn't stop staring at Mike. He rubbed his fore-head and his eyes, wishing he would wake up, that this bad dream would end. He'd started this day determined to fix his life—instead he'd wound up with his friend almost dying. And who knew what would happen to Mike now? Maybe he would be in a coma for the rest of his life. Maybe he would be a vegetable. Maybe Sam had been too late.

From: gaia13@alloymail.com
To: shred@alloymail.com
Time: 11:03 A.M.
Re: Good morning

Hey, Ed—
    So did you manage to get any sleep last night?
I have to say, when you told me about the whole
thing with Heather, I tried my best to deal with
it. But do you really think that going after her
is such a hot idea? She's hurt you. Needless to
say, she can be a bitch. But you know all this.
Anyway, write back. There's something I really
want to talk to you about.

                              G$

From: shred@alloymail.com
To: gaia13@alloymail.com
Time: 11:33 A.M.
Re: No sleep

G$—

   You should really give Heather a chance. You
don't know her. And who isn't a bitch at some
time or another? (That wasn't meant to be a dis,
even though it sounds like one. No offense.)
Anyway, I've hurt her, too. I know, I know—you're
probably wondering why I'm not being devastat-
ingly witty as usual. I guess I'm too depressed.
So what is it you wanted to tell me?

From: gaia13@alloymail.com
To: shred@alloymail.com
Re: No big deal
Time: 11:47 A.M.

Hey, Ed,

    Don't worry about it. And you're right about
the bitch thing. (No offense taken.) Just get
some sleep. We can talk later.

A huge chunk of brick and cement exploded on the ground with a deafening crash— less than two yards away from her. **her father's voice**

Surprise, Surprise

HOSPITAL MACHINE COFFEE WAS about one step up from horse piss, Sam realized. He swirled the scummy gray dregs of his third cup around in its plastic foam container. It probably wasn't the best thing to drink, considering the stress he was under. His stomach felt acidic, knotted with tension and fear.

He glanced around the emergency-room waiting area. He'd been here for about five hours already, but there were people who had been waiting longer than he had—people who hadn't seen a doctor yet. There was one young woman who kept puking into a plastic basin. Her skin was literally green. Her boyfriend kept complaining that she'd been here since this morning—pretty much to anyone who would listen. But still, the staff was too busy to see her. All around him, it seemed there was moaning. Children were crying fretfully or playing listlessly on the cold tiled floor. Talk about depressing. Did he really want to be premed and be faced with *this* every day of his life?

"Mr. Moon?" a strident voice called.

Sam turned to see an approaching African American woman in green surgical scrubs, a stethoscope hanging around her neck. She was flipping pages on a clipboard. She had a name tag: Dr. Burton.

"Yes?" Sam answered. He felt dizzy for a moment and realized he hadn't eaten anything all day.

"You came in with Michael Suarez?" the doctor asked.

"Yes." Sam swallowed. "How is he? Is he okay?"

"He's not great," she said matter-of-factly. "It looks like he's going to live, but we're not sure about any posttraumatic disability." She shot him a hard stare. "Have you called his parents?"

"Yes," said Sam, details swirling in his head. "They live in Florida. They're coming up as soon as they can. They'll probably be here late tonight."

"Good," said Dr. Burton. "And you've talked to the police?"

Sam shook his head, suddenly nervous. "No. What for?"

"They're going to want to talk to you about the drugs," she stated.

"But I had nothing to do—"

"Shhh," Dr. Burton soothed. "There's no reason to get upset. It's just procedure."

Sam took a deep breath and nodded. He glanced down at his cup. "Okay," he whispered. "I don't even know what he took. Was it heroin?"

"I'm afraid so," Dr. Burton said.

"He . . . stopped breathing for a while. Is he going to be—" Sam ran his hands through his hair.

"We don't know," Dr. Burton answered shortly. "But you saved his life. He's lucky you were there. You did everything right." She flashed him a tired smile. "Maybe you should consider med school."

Sam laughed hollowly. "Yeah, maybe. Can I see him?"

Dr. Burton shook her head. "I'm sorry, but hospital protocols dictate that we wait until his parents get here and give you permission. Why don't you go home, shower, eat something? Come back later, after his parents get here."

"Okay." Sam nodded.

Dr. Burton turned and strode back into the intensive care unit. All at once he was *sure* he'd never be able to be a doctor. No way could he carry himself with such calmness and detachment, surrounded by so much death and suffering every day. It took a certain kind of person—a very, very strong person. And intelligent. Not a sniveling little worm—

"Sam?"

He whirled around. *Oh my God*. The coffee cup nearly slipped from his fingers. He fumbled with it, splattering a few drops on the floor. He couldn't believe it. *Heather* was here.

"Did—did you . . . hear about Mike?" he stammered, baffled.

Heather frowned. "Who?"

Sam's eyes narrowed. "What are you doing here?"

A weary smile crossed her lips. "That's right. I forgot you didn't know."

"Know about what?" he asked, his heart bouncing.

"Phoebe's here. She has anorexia."

"Oh, my—" Sam broke off. He shook his head, then awkwardly reached for Heather's shoulder. But his hand fell before he made contact. Things were just too weird; he couldn't bring himself to touch her. Not *here* . . . not now. "I had no idea."

Heather shrugged. "I know. So who's Mike?"

"My suite mate, you know—Mike Suarez. He OD'd this morning."

"Jesus," Heather gasped. "I didn't know Mike did stuff like that."

"Me neither," said Sam. "He had a needle hanging out of his arm. And then he stopped breathing, and I did CPR. . . ." He shook his head. He felt removed and spacey, as if this were all happening on a blurred movie screen and he was standing apart from himself, watching.

"Oh my God. Sam, I'm so sorry. Will he be okay?"

Sam shrugged. "Dunno." Heather didn't look so great, now that he thought about it. For once her hair was a total mess. And her eyes were red and puffy, as if she'd been crying. But of course, that made sense. Her sister was in the hospital.

"You look beat," Heather remarked.

Sam managed a laugh. "I was just thinking the same thing about you."

Their gazes locked, then Heather turned away, staring at the floor. "Listen, Sam, it's actually a good thing I ran into you. We really need to talk. Can I come see you after school Monday?"

He nodded. "Sure."

"Good." Without looking at him, she turned and exited the hall, quickly and quietly. Sam watched her disappear. Once he wouldn't have let her leave without hugging her, kissing her, smoothing her hair. Now he couldn't even bring himself to lay a hand on her shoulder. He didn't know what was happening in her life. He didn't know a damn thing about her.

They were strangers. Complete strangers.

AFTER PLAYING A COUPLE OF CHESS

games in the park with her old friends Zolov and Mr. Haq, Gaia couldn't stand the cold anymore. How did these guys do it? Gaia had a pretty high pain threshold . . . but still. These guys were crazy. They were chess *addicts*.

"Where you go, Ceendy?" Zolov called after her as she hurried toward West Fourth Street. "You don't want nother game?"

Gaia just waved over her shoulder, laughing to herself. One of these days she would really have to tell Zolov that her name wasn't Cindy. He probably wouldn't believe it, though. The guy was ninety years old. People that old never believed anything new. They were set in their ways. It must be nice, she reflected, to be so certain of the truth. . . .

By walking fast, Gaia was able to warm up just a little bit. It was amazing how quickly the temperature plunged when the sun went down. Her eyes roamed over all the people in the park—mostly couples, walking and huddled together for warmth. She felt an odd pang of loneliness. Tonight she would eat alone . . . yet again. Unless Ella and George were home, of course. But she doubted they would be, and even if they *were*, there was no way Ella would want to sit at the same table as Gaia—not after nearly beating her senseless.

Too bad Ed wasn't available for dinner. He was going to the hospital to see Heather's sister—the one he'd once said he wanted to sleep with, back when Mary and Gaia and Ed were playing truth or dare. Now that girl was in the hospital, almost dead because she'd been trying to lose weight. Gaia swallowed. How did people get so messed up?

Turning down Perry Street, she saw that no lights

were on inside the Nivens' brownstone. Good. It looked like she had the place to herself. After a rousing dinner of Lucky Charms, she would go upstairs for a steaming bath, then finish her homework.

Five feet from the front door, Gaia paused to pull out her key. Then she froze. The hairs on the back of her neck stood on end.

"Watch out!" a voice shouted.

Dad? Gaia wondered, stunned, even as her reflexes took control and she dove for cover, rolling across the sidewalk to the curb. It sounded like his voice—

A huge chunk of brick and cement exploded on the ground with a deafening crash—less than two yards away from her. Gaia covered her head with her hands. Bits of stone stung her flesh. In less than a second, though, the shower of debris had ended. A thick cloud of dust settled over her.

What the hell was going on? Gaia took her arm from her face and scanned the area. No sign of her father. Was it really his voice? No. Impossible. She supposed it could have been her uncle's . . . but then, where was he? Her eyes flashed to the pile of broken rock next to her, then up at the Nivens' brownstone. Jesus. Squinting, she could make out the ragged, broken top of a chimney, right at the front of the building.

The chimney had fallen off the freaking house.

All of a sudden the front door burst open and George came huffing out, eyes wide. "Gaia!" he called.

His frightened gaze darted between her sprawled form and the pile. "What's happening? I was taking a nap, and I heard this noise. . . ." He crouched beside her. "Are you okay? What happened?"

Gaia sat up straight and pointed at the roof. "I think part of the chimney fell down," she murmured.

He followed her outstretched finger, breathing hard. His nose was already turning red from the cold. "Oh my God," he muttered. "How could that happen? We just had the roof repaired last fall."

"Beats the hell out of me," Gaia mumbled, brushing dust and grit off her jacket.

George helped her to her feet. "Are you all right? Oh, no, you have a cut on your cheek. It's a wonder you weren't killed."

Yes, it was a wonder. In a daze, Gaia let him lead her inside—straight to a bathroom. She stood still while he gently washed her cut and put some antiseptic lotion on it. Her mind was racing in a dozen different directions. She *had* heard somebody's voice. And that voice had sounded like her father's. But that was clearly her overactive imagination. Her father was gone—forever. And good riddance. But whoever had called to her had known that the chimney was falling. Why, though? Why would a chimney fall at the very moment Gaia was under it? It couldn't be a coincidence. No. She would have to check out the roof for herself.

She couldn't
be here.
Not in
school. But
she was.
She was
that sick.

scent
of
chalk

AS SOON AS ED WAS DONE WITH

high school, he never again wanted to be in a position where he had to get stuff out of metal lockers. He hated lockers. Everything about them was miserable: their color (gray), their smell (invariably like old

Fargo Sandwich

gym socks—even if you didn't *wear* gym socks), their sound (that depressing clang). No, he vowed never to see a locker again. Which, he supposed, ruled out occupations like peace officer, firefighter, personal fitness trainer. But that was fine. The wheelchair pretty much ruled out those same jobs, too.

The moment he closed his locker door on this particular Monday morning, however, he hated it for another reason. He hated it because it was *his*—and therefore it was reasonable for people to assume that he could be found next to it. People like Gaia and Heather, for instance: who were now approaching him from opposite ends of the hall. Cornering him. Catching him in the middle.

Shit. His head slumped. This was exactly the kind of situation he had been afraid of. Whenever those two got together, disaster inevitably followed. Besides, he knew that Heather was probably still pissed off at him. And when Heather was pissed off, *everyone* suffered. He should have called her yesterday. But he'd been expecting to see her at the hospital Saturday night when he'd gone to visit Phoebe. Unfortunately she'd already left. Phoebe had (very nobly) tried to smooth over the situation—telling him that Heather was head over heels in love with him, but still . . . this would be bad. He was sure of it.

Heather reached him first. Barely.

She folded her arms across her chest and glared at Gaia, then lowered her eyes to Ed. "We have to talk," she stated.

Ed swallowed. He offered Gaia a feeble smile, then glanced back at Heather. "Okay," he muttered. "Now?"

Heather nodded.

"Oh, hey, I saw Phoebe Saturday night," he found himself commenting stupidly. But he couldn't help it. The tension kept him from thinking straight. "She looked better."

"Yeah, for a skeleton," Heather muttered. She glanced up at Gaia again. "Do you mind? I'm trying to talk to Ed."

Gaia shrugged. "So am I."

Blood started rushing to Ed's face. Maybe he should just scoot out of here and leave these two alone. . . .

"Maybe we could all get together after school and have coffee," Gaia suggested sarcastically. "I know you love coffee."

Ouch. Ed bit his lip. He didn't know whether he wanted to laugh or run and hide. The first time Gaia met Heather, she'd spilled coffee all over her—and needless to say, the relationship worsened from there.

"Sorry, I can't," Heather said with false politeness. "I'm meeting *Sam* after school."

The name struck Ed like a punch in the gut. He whirled around, suddenly seething, forgetting all about Gaia and Heather's stupid problems with each other. What the hell was going on? Were Heather and Sam back together? After *everything*?

"I'm breaking up with him today," she added quietly, staring straight at Gaia.

Ed blinked. Well. Surprise number two. Again the world flipped over. "You are?" he asked—as he heard Gaia asking the exact same question at the exact same time.

"Yes," said Heather. She smirked, her steely eyes flashing between the two of them. "If that's okay with you two."

THINGS WERE GETTING BETTER, SAM

realized. Yes. Step one of his self-improvement plan was already in place. He clutched the graded lab report in both hands, smiling down at the bright red B. All it

The New Terms

took was a little extra focus, a little more concentration—and of course, the will to shut out everything else in his dismal life. But pretty soon he'd change the B to an A. He'd be back on track.

And later this very day he would initiate step two: breaking up with Heather.

For the first time in weeks he actually felt *in control*. He'd taken charge of himself. It was amazing how powerful that simple feeling could be.

"Okay, class, for Wednesday read chapter ten," Dr. Witchell called from the front of the classroom. "We'll be conducting experiments on Friday."

Sam nodded as he slung his backpack over one shoulder and pushed himself up from his cramped wooden chair. *Good,* he thought. More work. *Much* more work. He was actually looking forward to studying. Anything to take his mind off—

"Is your friend all right?"

He froze. Somebody was standing in the doorway.

Blood turned to ice in his veins. There was no way . . .

Ella smiled and stepped inside, allowing the rest of Sam's classmates to exit. Sam could only stand there and gape at her, petrified. No. She couldn't be here. Not in school. But she was. She was *that* sick.

Gradually everyone filed through the door. Ella's smile remained intact, her eyes fixed on Sam.

Dr. Witchell was the last one out. He stared at Ella, then shot Sam a confused glance. Sam would have done the same thing in his shoes. Sam was probably the only student who had ever had a beautiful, red-haired woman show up to greet him—decked out in a fur coat, no less.

"How's your friend?" Ella asked again once they were alone.

For a moment Sam couldn't breathe. In that instant he realized, with an appalling, stomach-dropping shock, that Ella must be referring to Mike. Which meant that she must have had something to do with his overdose.

"What do you know about it?" he hissed.

She didn't answer. She simply laughed. The sound of it was like the scrape of fingernails on a chalkboard.

Sam winced. He took a step forward. "You—"

"See ya later, alligator," Ella interrupted in a singsong voice. She darted out of the room, leaving him staring after her in horror. He wanted to catch up, to pin her against the wall, to demand that she tell him what she had done to Mike . . . but he couldn't move. Instead he collapsed against the wall, rubbing one hand through his hair. He was sweating, even though the classroom was cold.

Ella had almost killed Mike.

Which meant that Mike's OD was Sam's fault—all because Sam didn't want to sleep with Ella again. What was he going to do? What in God's name was he—

Actually, he knew the answer to that question.

Yes . . . he saw it now with perfect clarity. Ella had crossed the crucial line—the line where people's lives were at stake. And that meant Sam could stop her by any means necessary. *She* had set the new terms. He had no choice but to keep her from trying to kill again.

Whatever it took.

IT WAS AMAZING HOW EVOCATIVE

Odor Number Three

certain smells were. Baby powder—a specific brand—always made Tom think of the day he and Katia had first brought Gaia home from the hospital. God, she had been so passive. She'd hardly ever cried. And she was big even then, with plump little arms and such smooth skin. . . .

Luckily Tom hadn't been around baby powder in a long time. He didn't know if he'd be able to handle the flood of memories it would unleash. Now, fading back into an NYU classroom, Tom was assailed by the scent of chalk. It instantly brought him back to the academy, the training he'd undergone there.

Luckily that training had saved his precious daughter's life.

He still couldn't believe how close Gaia had come to getting killed. When he'd seen Ella climbing up the roof of the brownstone, he was sure that she'd found the bugs. And when she'd jimmied around with one of the chimneys, he'd assumed she was yanking off wires—destroying about fifty thousand dollars' worth of stolen CIA material in the process.

But no. She'd been trying to kill Gaia. *His* daughter.

He clenched his fists at his sides as he stood still in the sterile, deserted lecture hall—hesitating as Sam strode past the open doorway. He knew that from this day forward, the smell of bricks and concrete would remind him of betrayal.

But what was Ella really *up* to—aside from trying to kill Gaia? It seemed apparent (at least from Sam's body language and the few scraps of conversation Tom had overheard) that Sam was *not* happy to be involved with Ella. He was simply another one of her victims. Which meant, by extension, that he was another one of Loki's victims. Were Ella and Loki blackmailing

Sam in some way? Anything was possible. Oh, yes—after the stunt Ella had pulled Saturday, Tom knew that no act, no matter how depraved, was off-limits. Soon he would go to George. Soon he would tell George the truth.

But in the meantime he would corner Ella and acquire the concrete evidence he so desperately needed to prove her guilt.

"GAIA, THE HUMAN HOUSEFLY," ED

Exclusive Club of Two

remarked dryly.

Gaia frowned as she poured the fourth packet of sugar into her small coffee, then stirred the steaming liquid with a small plastic straw. "What do you mean?" she asked.

Across the booth, Ed raised his eyebrows. "I mean you eat more refined sugar than anyone I know," he said. "You should weigh three hundred pounds."

Gaia shrugged. The truth of the matter was that he was right. Her diet pretty much consisted of fat and sugar. But stress probably contributed to a lean figure. And she certainly had plenty of stress in her life. She glanced out the café window at the throng of pedestrians on Broadway. Judging from their hurried pace and all of the sour expressions, it seemed that *everyone* had a lot of stress in their life. But maybe it was just the cold. Whatever. This was New York City. Stress came with the territory.

"Hey, I'm just trying to make conversation," Ed said. "Just trying to keep things light. You know, considering that Heather is in Sam's dorm room right now."

As if we both needed reminding, Gaia thought bleakly. But that was Ed: always speaking the truth, no matter what the consequences. Sometimes it was refreshing. Other times it was extremely annoying.

"Do you think she'll break up with him?" Gaia asked. Now that Ed had broached the subject, there was no point in trying to pretend that neither of them was thinking about it.

Ed sighed. "That's what she said."

"I know," Gaia said, looking at him squarely. "How big of a liar is she?"

Frowning, Ed turned toward the window. "Um, usually not much of one, I think. She usually just lets rip with the truth." He snickered. "Kind of like you, actually."

Blech. She was actually being compared to Heather. She actually had something in *common* with Heather—besides her taste in men, of course. She took a sip of coffee. "So you think she's breaking up with him. Are you going to go out with her if she does?"

Ed turned back to her, his lips pursed. "Boy, you're really not holding anything back today, are you?"

Gaia shrugged again. What was the point of holding things back? They'd tried that system for the past four months, and it hadn't worked. If they were going to stay friends, there couldn't be any more secrets between them. Gaia understood that now. Besides, she was curious: about Ed's accident, about his breakup with Heather . . . about *everything*. Anyway, the more Gaia knew, the more she could help him, right?

Of course, Gaia still had no intention of telling Ed certain things about *her* life. But that was for his own safety. That was just common sense.

"I don't know if I'm going to go out with her," he said finally. "What about you and Sam? He'll finally be free—no more Heather. Will the lovely and determined Gaia Moore finally manage to shed her—"

"Shut up!" Gaia snapped.

Ed flinched slightly. His face went pale. "Jesus," he muttered.

Gaia swallowed, quickly glancing around to make sure no one was staring at her. All of a sudden she felt sick. What was her problem? Ed was just teasing her. Besides, he was asking a perfectly legitimate question, given the signals Gaia had sent him in the past. She'd pretty much confessed that her life's goal was to lose her virginity to Sam Moon. Ed had no idea that Sam was sleeping with her foster mother.

How could he? It was too foul, too ludicrous.

"Look . . . I'm sorry, Ed," she whispered, trying to smile. "I didn't mean to yell at you. It's just . . . I don't know. I'm kind of in a freaked-out state right now, you know?"

Ed nodded, his face relaxing a little. "Welcome to the club," he said glumly.

In desperation Gaia almost blurted out the news about her uncle, that she was meeting him for dinner tonight—just to talk about something else, *anything* . . . but once again she decided against it. Judging from Ed's faraway expression, she figured he was just too wrapped up in himself right now to listen to her. But that was fine. Ed deserved to be wrapped up in himself every once in a while.

AS HEATHER WALKED PASSED THE

guard—the doltish meathead who'd seen her come and go a hundred times—it finally occurred to her that this might very well be the last time she would ever set foot in Sam's dorm. She'd never see that guy again. He'd long

The Last Time

since stopped asking to see her ID. He knew her by sight. She swallowed, boarding the rickety elevator. For a while it had seemed like she practically lived here.

Now she felt like she was returning to the scene of a crime. In a way, she was. She'd committed a lot of crimes here: the crime of lying, the crime of pretending to be someone she wasn't—all to please Sam.

The elevator lurched to a halt on the fourth floor, and Heather strode briskly down the hall to Sam's suite. As usual, the door was wide open. She paused for a moment, suddenly remembering that Mike was in the hospital. No wonder it was so quiet around here. She stepped inside and saw Sam kneeling by the door to his bedroom, a cordless drill in his hand.

"Hey," she said quietly.

He glanced up at her and managed a smile. "Hey," he said. He looked better than he had Saturday; there was color in his cheeks, and his tousled brown hair was combed and clean.

Heather peered down at him. "What are you doing?"

"Putting a deadbolt lock on my door," he mumbled, standing up.

She laughed. "Finally," she mused. How many times had people barged in on them because of his stupid broken doorknob? His roommates, Gaia . . . All of a sudden she sobered. Thinking of Gaia reminded her why she was here. It wasn't to benefit from the new security system.

No. She sighed. It was time to get down to business.

"Want to come into my room?" he asked.

Heather nodded, feeling an uncomfortable twinge. Her breath came a little faster. Last time she'd been invited into Sam's room, they'd ended up having sex. The way a boyfriend and girlfriend were supposed to. But at the same time . . . not.

"Sorry about the mess," he apologized, stepping aside.

Yeah, right. If he were sorry, he would have cleaned. Heather took a whiff of the air and tried not to grimace. Yuck. It stank in here. Why was it that all boys lived like pigs? Well, actually, Ed no longer lived like a pig—but that was only because he couldn't. He *would* if he didn't have to worry about getting his wheels caught on something and being stuck. Scanning the room, Heather saw a bare spot on the end of Sam's bed and quickly sat down.

Sam remained standing in the doorway. Heather could still appreciate his cuteness, she realized—the way his bare feet jutted from under his jeans, and his shirt was only half buttoned and untucked. But she wasn't here to be nostalgic.

The seconds ticked by in silence.

"So," Sam said.

"Sam, I came here today for a reason," Heather blurted out. She stared down at her lap, then glanced up at him again.

He nodded thoughtfully. "I'm glad. We need to talk."

Heather bit her lip. She had to get this out now; otherwise she knew she'd never be able to go through with it. Already she could feel a strange heat in her chest. A lump was forming in her throat. "Can I go first, please?" she said in a strained voice.

"Uh . . . sure." Sam stepped across the mess on his floor and slouched down in his desk chair, his face unreadable. "Go ahead."

She took a deep breath, then looked at her hands again. "Sam, we've been going out for nine months now." *Oh, Jesus.* She was speaking in clichés again. Sam deserved better than that. "And . . . I mean, most of it's been great, you know? But sometimes . . . sometimes I think we've taken this thing about as far as it can go." The words sounded lame, ridiculous, childish. But how else could she express herself? Maybe she should have prepared a speech.

Sam leaned forward. His forehead wrinkled. "What do you mean?"

Heather smiled wistfully. But she couldn't bring herself to tear her eyes from her hands, still resting in her lap. "Sam, you're a great guy, and it's been wonderful—mostly—being with you. But we're just not right for each other. I'm sure you feel the same way. I mean, you know, lately things haven't been like they were when we first met."

He didn't say a word.

"It's just . . . I don't want to hurt you," Heather went on, to fill the silence. God, this was torture. "And I don't want to be hurt anymore, either."

"You want to break up," he stated suddenly.

Heather finally lifted her head. His tone wasn't angry, or recriminating, or even particularly sad. It was just . . . flat. Tired. As if he'd just run a marathon and now needed to rest. And in a way, Heather was very relieved. But in another way, she was mildly offended. Wouldn't he want to put up some kind of a fight?

Sam nodded, then stood and walked three steps to the window. His only view was the ugly back of a building twenty feet away, which blocked light and gave his room the feeling of a prison cell. His face remained blank. But how *should* he react to this? Maybe she secretly wanted him to start crying, to apologize—and she would cry, too, and he would feel like an asshole . . . and then they would end up in bed. *No.* Her lips tightened. That couldn't happen. She wouldn't allow herself to be weak.

"I'm not surprised," he said after a few seconds.

She blinked at him. "Are you angry?"

He shook his head, still gazing out the window at nothing. "I don't know what I am," he said. "Just confused, I guess." He glanced over his shoulder. "If you want to know the truth, I was going to break up with *you*."

Heather scowled. "Really?" she asked. She wasn't sure if she believed it. This was just a little too easy. Then again, Sam had always been honest with her. In fact, she owed it to him to be completely honest right now, too. *Completely.* "Well, I'm glad," she continued. "Because there's something I have to tell you. I . . . I think I'm in love with someone else."

Sam's eyes widened. He seemed to stop breathing.

"It sort of snuck up on me," Heather admitted. "I didn't expect it, wasn't looking for someone else. But it just grew and grew, and then . . ." Her voice trailed off, and once more she looked down at her hands.

"Are you telling me you've been seeing someone else?" Sam asked.

Heather shook her head. "Not exactly," she said. "But over the last couple of days, I realized that I really wasn't being fair to you."

Without warning, Sam stomped over to the door and threw it open. "Get out," he barked.

"What?" Heather gasped, flabbergasted.

"You heard me." He thrust an arm toward the hallway, averting his eyes. "Take a hike. I don't want to deal with this."

Heather's lips started trembling. "But I . . . I can't believe you're so mean," she choked out. "I mean, you practically told me you were in love with Gaia—"

"Get *out*, Heather," Sam commanded.

It took her a moment to realize that *he* was crying, too. But she didn't care. She pushed herself off his bed and stalked out into the common room. To think that she'd wanted to spare his feelings . . . Jesus. What an insensitive *jerk*. But then she froze and whirled to face him.

"For God's sake, Sam, what the hell did you want me to do?" she found herself screaming. "Of *course* I found someone else. You never call me; you're totally uninterested in my life. . . . I feel like a piece of gum you want to scrape off your shoe! So just get off it, and get over yourself! We're *over!*"

And with that, she turned and bolted. The last image she had of Sam was of his mouth hanging wide open in a look of utter shock. And she was glad.

Well. That hadn't been so hard, had it?

Have you ever felt like you were a complete stranger to yourself? Today I saw and heard myself acting like an asshole, and yet there seemed to be nothing I could do about it. I couldn't stop. I was utterly powerless. It was as if all the pressure and tension I felt over Ella and Gaia and school and Mike and Heather herself had reached critical mass—and then *kaboom!*—it exploded. All I needed was the match to set it off, the little spark. Conveniently Heather provided it.

So now phase two of my plan has been completed. Heather is now officially out of my life. Problem solved. Not exactly the way I'd planned it—but hey, beggars can't be choosers, right? Still, I can't believe that *I* got pissed because *she* was cheating on me. I guess I was humiliated. But what the hell have I been doing?

Which reminds me, that new

doorknob ought to keep Ella out
of my suite. That baby is as
solid as a rock. There's no way
I'm going to let Ella spike *me*
with a needle while I sleep. Damn
it, though. Heather was just trying to be cool, and I screwed it
up. We could have had a nice,
civilized talk, hugged one last
time, and both left feeling good
about each other. Instead she
hates me, and I'm disgusted with
myself.

So I guess phase two wasn't so
great after all.

I left Ed at five-thirty. It was already dark, and I swore at myself all the way from Astor Place to Sixth Avenue. I was supposed to go up on the Nivens' roof to check out why two hundred pounds of brick and cement narrowly avoided crushing me.

But I forgot all about it.

My brain feels so crowded lately. It's not like my life is simple most of the time—it isn't. I have one of the weirder lives I know. But lately it's almost impossible to have any downtime when my gut is twisting up about somebody in the orbit of my existence: Ella, Sam, Ed, Heather, Uncle Oliver . . . the guy who yelled at me yesterday.

Note to myself: Check roof tomorrow.

Gaia stared at him. This had to be a joke. A sick, **another** cruel joke. But he **woman** seemed to be dead serious.

MANY PEOPLE UNDERESTIMATED

The Right Look

Frederick's, in Ella's opinion. Sure, sometimes the quality of workmanship wasn't quite what it should be, and sometimes the fabrics were less than superior. But their designs were very fresh. Comfortable and practical. And Ella appreciated their designers' sense of humor. Ever since this store had opened on Fifty-seventh Street, Ella's wardrobe had grown dramatically. It was a treat to be able to come here, try things on, chat with the salespeople. And she'd met all kinds of interesting people. Not the kind that ran in George's boring Agency circles. No . . . the kind that led secret lives that were actually worth exploring.

As Ella examined a black cashmere bodysuit, she wondered what Sam would think of it. His eyes would pop. Any idea of resistance would fade from his mind. That was all she needed, really—the right *look*. She smiled to herself. Boys were so predictable—

"That would look stunning on you," a melodious female voice said.

Ella glanced up. A woman was standing beside her—a woman about her age, who had the most extraordinary topaz eyes. *Do I know you?* she wondered. Quickly Ella swept her from head to foot. The woman was dressed conservatively, in a gray, chalk-stripe business suit, white silk blouse, pearl choker. Her hair was in a bun: simple and elegant—and her face was fresh and unlined, with hardly any discernible makeup. Almost immediately Ella's curiosity waned. Aside from the woman's eyes, she appeared drab and dull. It was doubtful she had any excitement to offer.

"Really," the woman said. "Stunning."

Ella let the bodysuit trail through her fingers. "You think so?"

The woman nodded, a hint of a smile playing around her full lips. She glanced around the store. "I just love this stuff, don't you? It makes me feel so feminine."

Hmmm. Yes, Ella's curiosity was definitely slipping down the drain. *Feminine* was *not* the word Ella would use to describe this kind of clothing. For her, it was more empowering, more aggressive. Almost dominating.

Turning, she moved to another rack. Oh, well. It appeared that she wouldn't make any new friends today. But just as she glanced at a row of dresses, she caught a glimpse of the woman's skirt. A long slit had parted, revealing her leg up to her thigh—and Ella saw an expanse of black fishnet stocking, stopped midthigh by a black leather garter studded with tiny silver spikes. Her eyes widened. She couldn't help glancing up.

The woman was staring straight at her, smirking slightly. Her topaz eyes glittered.

Ella felt a twitter of excitement. It was as if this woman were sharing a dark secret, a secret meant only for them: *There's more to me than what the untrained eye can see.*

"Hi," Ella found herself saying. "My name's Ella."

"My name's Pearl," said the woman, smoothing her hands over her hips before offering one to Ella to shake. "Delightful to meet you."

"Yes," Ella murmured. "Perhaps it will be."

GAIA APPROACHED THE BROWNSTONE

cautiously, remaining in the street behind a line of parked cars until she was almost at the front door. Then she crouched for a few very cold seconds, surveying the area—checking out the roof for movement, listening intently. The sun had long since set.  In the darkness she heard and saw nothing. So it appeared that no chimneys would be falling on her— at least not today. She quickly scurried to the door and unlocked it, then slipped inside and slammed the door as fast as she could.

Jesus. How many kids had to run a security check before they walked into their own houses? How many kids had to live like this?

"Hi, Gaia," George called from the kitchen. "I'm whipping up some spaghetti. Are you hungry?"

Poor George. Tonight, clearly, he'd planned on having one of those painful meals where he actually tried to be a father. The guy's timing was terrible. So was his cooking, for that matter. Now Gaia was even *more* thankful to be meeting her uncle.

"Oh, gee, George," she answered as politely as she could. She tiptoed toward the stairwell, hoping she wouldn't have to face him. "I'm sorry. I'm eating dinner out tonight."

"Really?" He sounded disappointed. There was a clatter of dishes in the sink. "Ella's still out somewhere, and I was hoping you and I could have a chance to catch up on things. I know I've been working a lot lately."

Gaia hesitated, biting her lip. She didn't want to make life worse for George. He had it hard enough, living with that witch. But she couldn't blow off meeting Oliver. This was her chance to get out of this hellish place. If George were smart, he'd get out, too.

"I'm sorry," she said finally. "I made this date last week."

"A date?" His tone lightened. "Anyone I know?"

"No, not that kind of date," Gaia clarified, laughing. "It's just a friend." *And relative,* she added silently. *Hopefully someone who will set me free.*

"Oh. Well, some other time," George said. "I probably won't see you when you get back. I'm going out of town tonight, and I'll be back the day after tomorrow. But don't be out too late, okay? It's a school night."

"Okay," Gaia answered, escaping up the stairs to her lair. Something about the plaintive sound of George's voice sent a shudder of sadness through her. He was a lonely man—and a man who had no idea of how horrible his life really was. Maybe someday she would try to do something nice for him. In the meantime, however, she had her own problems to worry about.

"I'M HERE," SAID A VOICE.

"Busy tonight?" George asked. He leaned out into the hallway just to double-check that Gaia was upstairs.

"Just the usual," came the reply. "What's up?"

176

"I've got an odd feeling," said George quietly into the receiver. "I thought if you had a chance, you could keep an eye on yellow bird tonight."

"Something going down?" The voice sounded alert, tense. There was a slight clicking noise in the background.

"Not that I know of," George mumbled. "It's just a feeling."

"Sometimes feelings are all we can trust," said the voice.

George sighed. "Sometimes."

"I'll keep an eye on her."

"Thanks." George hung up just as Gaia thundered back down the stairs.

"Bye, George!" she called.

"Have a good time!" he called back. "Be careful!"

The door slammed.

For a moment George stood silently in the brightly lit kitchen, ruminating over thoughts, details, facts. Something was bothering him, some sound . . . a tiny click. Yes. While he'd been speaking just now. What *was* that? George looked at the phone—a white wall phone that had come with the house. George regularly ran a sweep of the whole brownstone, and he knew all the lines were secure. But there *had* been a click.

His face darkened. He was alive because he had listened to his gut a million times. Instinctively he took the handset off its hook and quickly unscrewed the mouthpiece. What he saw was so astonishing that he actually gasped out loud. There was a bug in the phone. A high-tech, professional bug. The kind the Agency used. Jesus.

On the stove, the spaghetti started to boil over.

GAIA COULD BARELY TOUCH HER

food. She was too restless, too insecure. Uncle Oliver had chosen another cozy, secluded restaurant—the Cloisters, in the West Village—but tonight the candlelit dining room was stifling. They'd already been here for almost half an hour, gone through

Here Today, Gone Tomorrow

their appetizers, drunk wine (which for some reason only made Gaia feel *more* anxious)—but Oliver hadn't brought up the idea of her moving in once. Instead they'd talked about school, the weather, New York . . . *anything* but what was on Gaia's mind. In other words, they'd bullshitted. And Gaia was getting tired of it.

"What's wrong?" he asked, peering over at her plate of lamb chops. His dark suit made a soft swishing sound whenever he moved. "Lost your appetite?"

Gaia shook her head. "I . . . I just." She closed her mouth. Was he waiting for *her* to bring it up? Or was he hoping she wouldn't so he could just forget about the whole thing? Maybe he'd gotten cold feet. Maybe tonight would be the last time she ever saw him. It certainly would be in keeping with the rest of the Moore family. Here today, gone tomorrow. And how could she blame him? He did secret work, traveled the world, wore stylish suits, knew everything. Maybe he even had a family somewhere. And a real daughter, not a screwed-up niece. But even if he didn't, the sad truth was that he was too glamorous for a freak like her. It was that simple—

"I've given a lot of thought to your question," he said suddenly.

She jerked. Her pulse immediately doubled. It was as if he'd read her mind.

A tired smile crossed his face. "It wouldn't be the simplest thing in the world," he stated, placing his silverware on the tablecloth and looking into her eyes. "You're still a minor. As foolish as that sounds, I would have to gain legal custody of you."

"I know," Gaia said, struggling in vain to keep the

desperation out of her voice. "But you're my *uncle*. Doesn't that mean anything?"

Oliver shrugged. "We would have to go to court and testify before a judge," he said. "It helps that I'm a family member, but unfortunately, your father probably signed a document stating that he intended you to live with the Nivens. His word would be hard to challenge."

Gaia nodded, feeling her heart sinking. The world turned black around her. To come this close, this tantalizingly close to escape . . . It just wasn't fair.

"I'm not saying that it's impossible," he soothed. "It'll just take some time. Would you be willing to make such a commitment?"

"Of *course*," she whispered, praying that she wouldn't do something idiotic like start crying. "I'll do whatever it takes."

Oliver smiled again, more easily this time. "Good," he said. "It's so nice to see such responsibility and maturity in a person so young." He hesitated for a moment, as if he were about to add something else, then shook his head.

"What is it?" she pressed.

"There is . . . one other option."

She nodded eagerly.

"Well, actually, it would be for both you and me simply to go away." He raised his eyebrows. "We could go live abroad. Legally you would be classified as a runaway, but that would only last until you're eighteen. Which is in August, if I remember correctly." He grinned. "The two of us could live in South America or Europe; wherever we want. We could travel from place to place. Then, once you are eighteen, everything would be legal . . . and we could settle back in the States. Or anyplace else, for that matter."

Gaia stared at him. This had to be a joke. A sick, cruel joke. But her uncle seemed to be dead serious.

"You mean . . . leave in the middle of the school year?" Gaia finally asked. Of course, she'd pretty much dropped out, anyway. The only thing that kept her going back was seeing Ed.

"Pah!" He waved his hand impatiently. "You are probably learning nothing. You're much too advanced for a local high school. You should be learning from the school of life. If you are traveling to the world's most beautiful places, seeing great works of art, seeing where history took place, living in different cultures . . . wouldn't that be a better education than what you're receiving at the hands of a bunch of lightweight bureaucrats?"

Gaia laughed. The dread that had all but consumed her suddenly transformed into euphoria. She couldn't believe it. Ha! If her principal could see her now . . . It was amazing. Her uncle had practically read her thoughts. School *was* a waste of time, at least this particular school. She and her uncle had more in common than she'd ever dreamed. Her mind began to race. She felt like she was about to burst right out of her chair. The idea was too overwhelming to take in all at once. Just picking up and leaving now, leaving everything behind: Ella, George, Sam, Heather . . . Ed. Okay, *that* would suck. But that was pretty much the only thing. Besides, she could get back in touch with Ed when she was eighteen. And she could always write letters, make phone calls, send e-mails . . . Damn. To pack up and take off, to get on a plane with her uncle, to go to new and exciting places—doing whatever she wished, living freely . . .

"It sounds incredible," she said slowly.

Uncle Oliver raised his hands. "I know it's a lot to think about right now. It's just a thought that occurred to me, and I wanted to put it out on the table. You take your time and think it through. The only thing is, if we decide to do it, we can't really change our minds—at least, not until you turn eighteen."

Gaia shook her head. Did he really think she had any doubts at all? He had to be kidding. "But what would you do overseas?" she asked. "What about your job?"

Uncle Oliver shook his head dismissively. "I can work pretty much wherever I go. My company has offices all over, and they're very flexible about accommodating me."

"Wow," Gaia said. The word was lame, but it was all she could manage. Her heart rattled like a jackhammer.

Uncle Oliver smiled, and just for the first time ever, Gaia saw *him*—just him and not the ghostly reflection of her father. He'd changed tonight . . . at least in her eyes. He *wasn't* her father. No, he had nothing to do with Tom Moore. He was her uncle. Her very own uncle. Her blood relative. And in her mind, she and Uncle Oliver were already on a plane together, toasting each other as New York City fell away behind them.

"CAN I GET YOU SOMETHING, ED?"

Boy of the Future

Heather's father asked jovially. "Soda? Water? Tea?"

"No, thank you," Ed said. "I'm fine."

Heather stared at Ed as he sat in her kitchen, unable to believe how composed and collected he was. But then, Ed had always been a class act when it came to impressing older people. He was just always so relaxed, so natural. He never tried to put on a front. And he never tried to kiss anyone's ass. He *earned* the respect of adults. A smile crept across Heather's lips. She was proud to have him here again—proud to be able to show him off with nothing to hold her back. Sam Moon was a thing of the past. Ed Fargo was the boy of the future.

"Okay, then, I'll leave you two kids to your studying," her father said. He headed back into the living room.

Ed grinned at Heather.

She smiled back and wordlessly led the way down the short hall to her bedroom. His wheels made no sound on the hallway floor. She'd been surprised when Ed had called after dinner, asking to come see her. And the truth of the matter was that she'd been too weak to say no. She hadn't been sure if she felt like dealing with him—not so soon after the whole Sam disaster—but now that he was here . . . she *definitely* didn't regret her decision.

"Too bad I forgot my books," Ed whispered as she opened her bedroom door.

She giggled, then turned and frowned at him, putting a finger over her lips to indicate silence. Ed rolled in ahead of her. She closed the door behind them, then turned on the light and sat on her bed.

"I have something for you," he said.

Heather raised her eyebrows. "Oh, yeah?"

"This is yours," Ed said, `pulling a bra out from his jacket pocket.` He had a perfectly straight face.

Her jaw dropped, and instantly she blushed. *Oh, Jesus.* She quickly lurched forward and snatched it from him. She'd known she must have left it behind that night, but it was still mortifying to have the evidence of her actions right here in front of her. Somehow it made her feel weak, vulnerable.

"Thanks," she muttered. "Your mom didn't find it, right?"

Ed shook his head. "Nope."

"Whew."

"So, anyway," Ed said pointedly. "How are you?"

She shot him a sharp glance, then collapsed back on her bed. Never one to beat around the bush, was he? "I'm . . . kind of a mess," she admitted, closing her eyes.

Ed said nothing.

"Yes, Ed," she grumbled. "I broke up with him."

"How was it?" he asked gently.

"It was weird. Bad. He acted like I was breaking his heart, like I had been two-timing him." She opened her eyes and stared up at the ceiling. Even the memories were making her nauseated. "He was a jerk."

Ed let out a deep breath. "Did you tell him about us?"

She swallowed, suddenly frightened of where this conversation was heading. Would they get into another fight? She didn't know if she could handle that. She only wanted everything to be okay, to *forget*. . . .

"Sort of," she said finally.

For a long moment Ed was quiet again. "Well, I'm glad you broke up with him," he said eventually.

"Me too," Heather whispered. God, it *was* a relief. She'd been banging her head against that wall long enough. He'd been totally obsessed with Gaia, anyway. "I always felt like second-best," she added. Maybe she shouldn't have admitted that last part—but by acknowledging her weaknesses, she would show him he had nothing to fear from her. Not anymore.

"No one could ever think you were second-best," Ed whispered. His voice was strained, hoarse.

Heather bit her lip. All she wanted right now was to lie in Ed's arms, have him hold her, feel his heart beating beneath his chest. And as if in answer to her silent prayer, Ed pushed his coat to the floor and rolled closer to her until their knees were touching. She sat up straight and looked into his eyes. Those deep, soft, sensitive eyes. He reached out and stroked her arm. She sat very still. Then she lowered her head gently and met his mouth with hers, and she felt so happy that she wanted to cry.

THE TINY, INFRARED BINOCULARS

Consumed by Crime

were pressed so firmly against Tom's face that his eye sockets were starting to ache. But he couldn't tear himself from the awful vision before him. Through the stained glass of the Cloisters' front window, he saw his brother reach out and touch Gaia's hand. He saw Gaia smile—her face blooming like a flower, her crystalline blue eyes glowing like stars as she gazed happily into the face of the man who Tom hated most in the world. His brother. His twin. His nemesis.

A bitter, acrid taste rose in the back of Tom's throat. He swallowed, shivering—but not from the cold. Loki and Gaia. Together. Since the murder of his wife five years before, Tom had gone to inconceivable lengths to keep Gaia safe and out of harm's way. He had even forsaken his relationship with her—cut off contact with his only daughter, his jewel, his only living link to Katia, in order for her not to be drawn into the web of deceit and betrayal that had taken Katia's life. To find her now, being lured into the tiger's lair so effortlessly, was more than he could handle.

Maybe he should just end it now. Maybe he should just burst into that restaurant and pump a bullet into Loki's brain. It would be so easy—

No! He almost said the word out loud. He had to control himself. If he did something rash, he would lose Gaia forever. No . . . he had to plan his moves perfectly, strategically. It was like a game of chess—only far more intricate and devious.

He saw Loki's lips move, saw Gaia nodding, looking . . . what? Hopeful? Excited? Intrigued? What was Loki suggesting to her? These last few days Tom had been so concerned about the immediate threat that Ella posed to Gaia that he hadn't stepped back to consider the big picture. But did Loki want Gaia dead? It certainly didn't seem as if he did. No, as George had told him, Loki wanted Gaia for himself. So why was Ella trying to kill Gaia? Was it possible that Ella was trying to trick Loki? That she had betrayed him in some way?

The questions squirmed in his mind again and again. He had underestimated his brother. But he'd done it for the last time. The moment was drawing near. Tom had known it would have to come sometime.

For his entire adult life, in fact, he'd known that he and Loki would face each other one day—and that one of them would have to die. When Loki had gone underground for so many years, Tom had hoped he'd somehow disappeared for good . . . been killed, been consumed by crime.

But then Loki had surfaced, and Katia had been murdered. And now Loki had come back for Gaia— the child Loki had always hoped he'd have with Katia.

The child Katia would never have allowed to be born.

Tiredly Tom lowered the binoculars and rubbed his eyes. Soon this game would end. Tom would see to that. It would end . . . and Tom and Gaia would never have to worry about Loki or the ghosts of the past ever again.

One More for the Road . . .

"YOU DON'T HAVE TO GO," PEARL said coaxingly.

"I do," Ella said. She tried frowning but ended up giggling instead. She couldn't remember the last time she'd been so relaxed and comfortable. Her head felt perfectly numb. She and Pearl had been sitting in a small, cozy wine bar (Ella was actually surprised she'd never heard of it) for the better part of four hours now, and Ella knew there was something she was supposed to do but couldn't think what. "This wine has gone straight to my head," she confessed. "Usually it doesn't affect me so much."

For some reason, Pearl started laughing. So did Ella. Before she knew it, the two of them were in hysterics, leaning together on the small velvet couch.

"Shhh!" Ella whispered, unable to control herself. She felt like a schoolgirl.

Finally Pearl took a deep breath. "I think the only solution is to have some more." She refilled Ella's glass again with the dark red liquid. In the dim light of this secluded corner, the wine glowed like rich velvet.

A few last giggles escaped Ella's lips, and she took a sip. Each glass was better than the last. "Oh, this is so good," she whispered, settling back against the couch. "I wish I didn't have to go, but I do. I just can't remember why." She bit her lip to keep from laughing. She couldn't believe how *wrong* she'd been about Pearl at first. Pearl might look conservative, but she wasn't at all. And it was so much more relaxing to be with another woman, a woman on her level, than to be with some stupid man or some enraging teenager. She *needed* easy, comfortable times like this. Even Pearl's *name* was perfect: a hidden jewel, something wonderful that you discovered only after you had peeled away layers of protection.

"Let me order another bottle," Pearl suggested. She rested her hand on Ella's shoulder.

"No, no, I have to go," Ella said again, looking deep into Pearl's warm topaz eyes, shining now with wine and candlelight. But the longer she thought about it, the more fuzzy her mind became. Why did she *have* to leave, anyway?

To go kill Gaia, an inner voice replied.

The thought seemed so absurd that she started laughing again. To leave this lovely, warm, comfortable, intimate scene just to go take care of that stupid brat . . .

"What's funny?" Pearl asked softly.

"Nothing," Ella said, taking another sip of wine.

"So are you going to stay?" Pearl pressed. Her fingers lingered on Ella's shoulder.

"I want to," Ella said. "I guess I should call my husba—oh, no!"

"What?"

Ella suddenly bolted upright, swishing the wine in her glass. "My husband went out of town tonight, and I was supposed to see him before he left. What time is it?"

Pearl checked her tiny gold watch. "A little after ten."

"Damn." Ella gathered up her coat, irritation flowing through her veins and counteracting some of the effects of the wine. She put her glass on the low coffee table, then slid her purse over one arm and rose unsteadily to her feet, teetering for a moment on her heels. "I'm sorry, Pearl, I have to go."

Pearl arched her eyebrows. "If you must . . ."

"I must."

"Just finish this, then," Pearl said, handing Ella her glass once more. "It will keep you warm out in the night air."

Ella hesitated, then thought, *What the hell?* She was already buzzed. She accepted the wine from Pearl's hands and took a deep sip. She wrinkled her nose. For some reason, it tasted heavy, sour. Maybe it was just tainted by the thought of going to see her husband and foster daughter. "I can't even enjoy it anymore," she complained.

"Oh, come on," Pearl coaxed in a seductive tone. As if to demonstrate, she picked up her own wineglass and drained its contents, her smooth throat working as the liquid went down. Ella watched, mesmerized, but shook her head regretfully.

"I—I have to leave," she stammered. She buttoned up her coat and started toward the door.

"Wait," Pearl called. "Do you want to meet me tomorrow?"

Ella hesitated, glancing over her shoulder.

"Come to La Cocina, in the West Village," Pearl said with an inviting smile. "Do you know it?"

"Yes." Ella stared into the topaz eyes.

"Then meet me there. Promise."

Ella nodded. "I promise."

"Nine o'clock." Pearl's voice was like music.

"La Cocina, nine o'clock," Ella repeated as she swayed slightly. Yes, she would be there. She would *definitely* be there.

IN SOME WAYS IT WAS EASIER

Unanswerable Question

for Ed to be with Heather here—in *her* house, with her parents right down the hall—than it had been back in Ed's house when they were alone. They couldn't just rip off their clothes and throw themselves on the bed. They couldn't get themselves in too deep right now, and maybe that was a good thing.

Ed just needed to keep telling himself that. Right now his lower back was killing him from leaning forward at this angle for so long—but he didn't want to stop kissing Heather. It just felt too good, too perfect.

There was a noise in the hall: the sound of a closing door. Ed jumped a little, pulling back.

Heather smirked. "Relax," she whispered. "It's just Dad. He'd never come in here without knocking. He probably just went to get his slippers or something."

Ed nodded but didn't make a move to pick up where they had just left off.

"Heather?" he heard himself ask. "What are we doing?"

She sighed and lifted her shoulders, smiling sadly.

"I don't know, either," he admitted. "Getting to know each other again?"

"Something like that." Her eyes searched his face. "Maybe we're moving a little fast," she said hesitantly.

He raised his eyebrows. "Maybe we're not moving fast enough," he joked. But Heather didn't smile. He could feel the air thicken with tension, as if a thick, poisonous smog were slowly filling the room, choking them. Too many issues had been left unaddressed. Sam. Gaia. The accident ...

"Maybe we *should* do some studying," Heather murmured.

Ed nodded.

Heather pushed herself off her bed, then began

pacing around the room—agitatedly, running her hands through her hair. Ed didn't move. Not that there was really a place for him to go. He could either spin in a circle or pop a wheelie. All at once his wheelchair felt bulky, awkward. It was too big for such a small space. It was in the way. *He* was in the way. Or was that just in his mind? Heather *wanted* him here. She didn't care about the freaking chair. That's what she'd been trying to tell him all week. So why was he still afraid, still unsure, still feeling inadequate? A voice was screaming in his skull: *Say something, you moron! Tell her how happy you are.* But he couldn't. That would be a lie. And he had no idea why.

"Ed?" Heather suddenly whispered. Her voice was shaking.

"Yes?"

"Do you still blame *me*?"

He bit his lip. That was the question, wasn't it? It was the only question in the end. And it had a thousand answers, an answer for every day he lived with paralysis: yes, no, not really . . . He couldn't bring himself to speak. He didn't know what he would say even if he could.

Heather marched to the door and opened it.

"It's been nice studying with you," she said as tears spilled from her eyelashes. "I'll see you later, okay?"

Ed nodded, then picked up his jacket and rolled into the hall. The real tragedy wasn't that he'd hurt Heather—although he honestly didn't mean to cause her any more pain. No, the real tragedy was that he knew he'd never be able to give her an answer. Ever.

ELLA STUMBLED A BIT AS SHE LET

herself in the front door of the brownstone. It was pitch black in here. But that was a good thing. It meant that George had already left. It meant that she wouldn't have to deal with his insufferable puppy dog eyes—or even worse, his anger. But thankfully, that was a relatively new development. She stuck out her hands into the abyss, groping for the light switch like a blind person.

A blind drunk person, she thought.

She laughed out loud. The sound echoed off the cold walls of the house. She was still pretty tipsy, wasn't she? All of a sudden her fingers bumped into the wall. After a few unsuccessful swipes she found the switch and flicked it.

Whoa. That light was pretty damn bright. Brighter than she remembered. She shambled into the living room to pour herself one last drink. Sure, she'd probably be hungover tomorrow . . . but she knew she wouldn't be able to sleep tonight without a nightcap. She was too wound up. The memory of Pearl clung to her like a fuzzy blanket. She smiled as she crouched beside the oak wet bar and opened the doors. God, why couldn't she meet more women like Pearl? Women of *her* caliber, *her* intelligence? Ella knew she needed to get out more. She'd been playing this bubblehead act far too long.

So what was she in the mood for? The bottles and crystal decanters swam before her eyes. So many options; so much fine liquor. There was *one* thing she would miss about this place. The luxury. But then again, Loki had expensive tastes, too. He'd keep her happy. Finally she decided on scotch. She sloshed some into a tumbler, then stood—a little too fast. Her head swam. She nearly keeled over. Laughing, she managed to grab onto the top of the wet bar. She didn't even spill.

"Here's to me," she whispered out loud, toasting herself in the empty house. She took a quick belt, wincing as the fiery liquid coursed down her throat. "May the living hell that is my life end soon—"

The front door clicked. Ella's eyes shot to the hall.

The latch was turning. *Oh, shit.* Had George forgotten something? This was all she needed. . . .

But her blood went cold the moment she saw the tall figure with the long, fairy-tale blond hair. Of course. She should have known.

"It's you," Ella spat, unable and unwilling to keep the disgust out of her voice. If Ella had played her cards right, the little brat would have been dead by now. But miraculously Gaia had managed to jump out of the way of the falling chimney. Those reflexes were sharper than Ella had guessed.

"Nice to see you, too," Gaia muttered.

Ella frowned. That was it? She had to admit, she was a little disappointed. She'd been expecting more anger, more rage. After all, the last time they'd seen each other, they'd both left with cuts and bruises. But Gaia didn't even seem particularly bothered. She simply headed upstairs.

"Hol' it right there!" Ella barked. Her words were slightly slurred. But she couldn't care less. She was drunk and pissed off. She wouldn't let Gaia get away with a little snide comment like that and not have to answer for it. . . .

"What, Ella?" Gaia asked flatly.

Ella lumbered out into the hall. "Where the hell have you been?"

Gaia paused on the stairs. She cocked an eyebrow and smirked at the glass in Ella's hand. "Well, I haven't been out drinking," she said sarcastically. "Unlike some people."

Ella's eyes burned. Her jaw tightened. "You little . . ." Without a moment's thought she tossed her drink in Gaia's face: *splat!*

Gaia's mouth fell open.

Brown liquid dripped from her porcelain features and onto the carpet. She blinked a few times and wiped her face with her sleeve. Her eyes narrowed.

"You bitch," she whispered.

Ella started to smile—until Gaia jumped off the stairs and pounced on her with an overhand karate chop to the shoulder. Unfortunately the booze had impaired Ella's reflexes. Normally she would have been able to block that strike, but instead it connected—and connected painfully. She dropped the tumbler and staggered. Shards of glass exploded across the floor. But before she had a chance to orient herself and regain her balance, Gaia lashed out again—this time with a kick to the stomach.

The breath exploded from Ella's lungs. She collapsed onto the floor—clutching her belly, writhing, eyes bulging. Hot desperation consumed her. She couldn't breathe! She felt like she was drowning. . . . *Damn it!* She was squirming like a worm, unable to control herself. How could she have been so careless? She *knew* Gaia was a good fighter. A sickening nausea began to rise in her guts, creeping up to her throat. All the booze, no doubt. With every ounce of energy she focused on not vomiting. That would be just a little *too* humiliating.

Gaia stood over her, breathing heavily. "You're shit faced, Ella," she said with maddening calm. "So I forgive you. Now, can I go upstairs?"

Ella tried to hurl an insult at her, but all she managed was a pathetic, wheezing gasp. She rolled over. Bad idea. Broken glass sliced into her sides, puncturing the skin. She glanced down and saw that she was bleeding from at least four different cuts. The blood was a deep, almost blackish red.

"Better clean that up," Gaia muttered, then turned and clomped up the stairs in those hideous construction worker boots.

Gathering all her strength, Ella forced herself to sit up straight. She finally managed to catch her breath. "No wonder Sam doesn't love you!" she shouted hoarsely, lashing out with the most powerful ammo she had. She wanted to *hurt* Gaia now—hurt the girl down to her very soul. "You're more man than woman!"

Gaia paused on the top step, then glanced over her shoulder. "Tell you what," she said—evenly, tonelessly. "If Sam loves you so much, then you and he can have my room. Because I won't be living in this house much longer. I'm going to go live with my uncle. He's taking me away from here. And he'll make sure I never have to look at either of your sick faces again in my life."

Uncle? Whatever pain Ella felt at being kicked in the stomach, it didn't compared to the utter horror she felt now. All at once she started gagging, choking back her own vomit. So that's what Gaia's cozy little dinner with Loki had been about. Loki was planning on fleeing with Gaia. And Ella wasn't part of the equation. It was a good thing she was so drunk right now. Because there was no way she could deal with this revelation sober. All those years, toiling away in this house for Loki's sake . . . all those years had been a lie. He'd been manipulating her the way he manipulated everyone else. And she'd been too blind with awe and love to see it.

The ultimate betrayal.

Ella sat amid the broken glass. *Think, think!* she cried to herself. Far upstairs, Gaia opened the door to her room and clomped around some more. Ella supposed she *could* just get her gun right now, march up there, and pump several holes into Loki's newest prize—thereby ending everyone's misery once and for all. But the sad truth of the matter was that she didn't think she could make it up to the top floor. She was too hurt, too drunk . . . too exhausted. Besides, Gaia wasn't going anywhere tonight.

No, Ella would take care of Gaia tomorrow. Blackness crept up on the corners of her vision, slowly enveloping her. The brownstone faded to nothingness.

Right now, she needed to sleep.

After four months I've finally sort of gotten used to Ed hanging on me like a coat on a rack. Meeting me in the hallway between classes. Asking me for coffee after school. Persuading me to ditch the school lunch and go for doughnuts somewhere.

Now the only question in his life seems to be: to Heather or not to Heather? And I hate to admit it, but I actually miss him. Already. And the thing that really bites about the whole situation is that I still haven't told him about my uncle. He has no idea that I even *have* an uncle. So, obviously he has no idea that I've decided to go for option number two. Leaving town. Living on the lam.

That's right. I've thought about it and thought about it, and I really have no choice. Especially after that pathetic little incident with Ella in the front hall. I can't go on

living like this. There's
nothing for me here. School is
a waste. I figured *that* out
last week. I knew it at dinner:
There's nothing to hold on to
in New York except Ed. Of
course, in an ideal world I
would have both Ed *and* Uncle
Oliver. And I would finally
figure out what the deal is
between Sam Moon and me . . .

Actually, in an ideal world I
would still be living the boring life of a suburban teenager
with both parents in upstate
New York. But let's not change
the subject.

Anyway. Ed is the only thing
I'll miss from my life here. That
and Krispy Kreme doughnuts. But
who knows? Maybe I'll be able to
dig up some of those in Europe or
South America or wherever else I
end up.

In a way, I almost hope Ed and
Heather do get together because
that will make it easier for me
to leave. I'll know he needs me

so much less. Because he has her.
And I will have Uncle Oliver.
This is my destiny: to be part of
a family.

   And then we'll all be happy.
Right?

With her thumb, she clicked off the safety. A tingle of anticipation shot down her spine. This moment had been a long time coming.

here and now

FOR THE FIRST TIME IN A LONG
while the weather was actually
warm enough to make chess in
the park tolerable. So as soon as
the final bell rang, Gaia headed
straight for her old tables in Washington Square. She
didn't even know why she bothered *going* to school
that day. Well, actually that wasn't quite true. She had
to go *somewhere*—at least to get the hell
out of the house. And the thought of spending
all day in a coffee shop or a diner just didn't sound
appealing. Besides, she was pretty much broke. She
couldn't afford to eat anything but cafeteria food. And
she'd wanted to see Ed, too, of course.

Luckily Ella had still been passed out on the front
hall floor this morning. Gaia had merely stepped over
her and left. Of course, Gaia had also entertained a
fantasy about sweeping up the broken glass and mop-
ping up the dried blood and putting all the garbage
into a huge plastic bag—with Ella, too, obviously—
and tossing everything in a Dumpster. But no . . . that
was too petty and would take too much effort. Ella
would be out of her life soon enough.

"Hello, Ceendy!" Zolov cried as Gaia approached.

Gaia waved, then quickly stuck her hand back in
her coat pocket, squinting in the harsh afternoon sunlight. As usual, Zolov was facing off against Mr.
Haq–and as usual, Zolov's ever present red-helmeted

208

Mighty Morphin Power Ranger sat by the side of the board. A strange, wistful feeling passed through Gaia's chest as she stared at it. Depending on when Oliver wanted to leave, this might very well be the last time that she saw Zolov and Mr. Haq . . . that she came here to play. It was sad, in a way.

But not *that* sad.

"Looks like Mr. Haq's got you cornered," Gaia said as she stood over them.

Zolov sneered. "Ha! I beat him. You see. I beat everyone."

Gaia laughed—then froze. Wait. What was that? The hairs on the back of her neck stood up, and she sharpened her gaze. That flash of burgundy. Across the park, among the crowd . . . There was no mistaking it. Gaia followed it with her eyes. Her fists clenched at her sides. It was her, all right. Ella. She was moving fast down a park path and toward Waverly. So she'd managed to haul herself off the floor. But what was she doing *here*?

And then it struck her.

Yes. *Duh.* Ella was on her way to see her little boy toy, Sam Moon.

". . . next game, Ceendy?" Zolov was asking.

Gaia blinked and shook her head, but she couldn't tear her gaze from Ella. "Huh? I'm sorry, what?"

"Do you want next game?"

"No, thanks," she answered, and found herself

leaving the table—chasing after the woman she so hated. She had some unfinished business to attend to. Yes. She had to confront Ella and Sam together. She had to see it with her own eyes.

And then she'd never have to see them again.

THE PLAN WAS WORKING PERFECTLY.

Using a car's passenger-side window as a mirror, Ella scanned the park behind her. Sure enough, Gaia was following her—and closing fast.

No doubt the little bitch figured that Ella was going to meet Sam. Just as Ella had intended.

Gaia's pathetic predictability was about the only thing that could make Ella feel better right now. Painkillers certainly weren't working—and she'd taken several different brands, both prescription and non-prescription. When her eyes had popped open about two hours ago, she'd experienced such an instantaneous, overwhelming wave of agony that she'd actually been *scared*. And the agony came from more than one source. Her brain was swollen, several sizes too big for her skull. Her stomach was burning, raw. Food had been impossible. And then there had been the broken glass in which she'd found herself lying. Some of it had cut her pretty deeply. She was still bleeding, in fact. She would probably need stitches.

But first she had to dispose of Gaia.

Besides, she could handle pain. Even the pain of being betrayed by Loki. Of being *used*. Of sacrificing everything for him, only to be discarded like a piece of broken or obsolete equipment. She knew now that in his eyes, she was exactly that. But still, she could handle it. He would suffer plenty when Gaia no longer existed.

Yes, pain was controllable—as was Gaia, much to her delight. Ella swallowed, her throat still dry, as she crossed the street. Each step sent another wave of queasiness through her body. But she didn't mind. She shot another quick glance at the window of a parked car; Gaia was now probably less than fifteen feet behind her. This was ridiculously easy. Ella slipped her hand into her open shoulder bag. Her fingers brushed against the cold steel of the silencer, screwed tightly into her thirty-eight-caliber pistol. A smile spread across her face. There was something undeniably sexy about a gun. There was power, mystique.

With her thumb, she clicked off the safety. A tingle of anticipation shot down her spine. This moment had been a long time coming. *Too* long.

She hesitated for a moment on the opposite side of the street. The sun was at a low angle—bright, glaring, disorienting. Night was preferable, but Ella could wait no longer. Anyway, the risk was minimal. Nobody was looking at her. The streets were relatively empty, as was the park. And there was a convenient little alley where she could duck after the deed was finished. Within seconds she would lose the gun, slip on a wig, and emerge on Eighth Street . . . a different person, with no idea of the murder that had just been committed. A visit to her trusty plastic surgeon would complete the transformation. And victory would be hers.

THE MOMENT TOM SAW ELLA DIP

her hand in her purse, he broke into a sprint—nearly barreling over several people in the park. Gaia was so close to her now. His legs pumped furiously. The two of them were still so far away. *Damn.* Why was Gaia following her?

He should have somehow gotten word to her that Ella had tried to kill her, that Ella was responsible for the falling chimney . . . that Ella was far more twisted than Gaia could ever suspect. Adrenaline coursed his system. He reached into his coat pocket and gripped his pistol. All his senses were alert, on hyperdrive. Every instinct told him something bad was about to happen right here, right now. The only question was whether he would be able to affect the outcome at all.

He was about twenty yards away. The sun was setting fast, and already the shadows beneath the trees were deeper, longer, darker. He peered ahead, trying to see through the undergrowth as Gaia crossed the street.

God, no.

It was at that moment that Ella suddenly stopped, pivoted, and turned on Gaia.

Sixth Sense

EVEN BEFORE GAIA SAW THE GUN

in Ella's hand, she sensed danger. The moment Ella had pivoted, in fact, Gaia made a split decision to dive to the left, rolling across the street beside the wheels of a parked van.

Thwip!

The dull pop of a silencer was as recognizable to her

as the sound of her name. In a way, it was like hearing an old song from the distant past. The last time she'd seen or heard a silencer was back in the Berkshires, when her father had showed her how to use one—

Thwip! Thwip!

Gaia felt a whizzing at her ear—and one of the tires began to deflate. There was no time to think. Relying on her years of honed training, Gaia went into survival mode. She jumped up and ducked behind the van, then crouched on the sidewalk. It was finally happening. Ella had finally lost her mind. But Gaia would worry about Ella's motives later. Right now, she had to disarm her.

An air of detached calmness settled over Gaia. She was perfectly focused on the moment—on the here and now. Peering under the body of the van, she saw Ella's boots, tiptoeing slowly. Gaia knew she couldn't hide forever; it was a game of cat and mouse that would inevitably end in her death. She needed a plan. Her eyes quickly scanned the sidewalk. They zeroed in on a rock. Gaia snatched it up and quickly threw it to her left.

The instant it hit the ground, Ella broke into a run—straight toward the sound—as did Gaia. Her plan was simple: to barrel straight into Ella before she had a chance to aim again. She could hear Ella's boots clicking on the ground as they both rounded the van, closer and closer to each other. One more second—

Smack!

Gaia collided with Ella, skull to skull, and they both went staggering. But surprisingly, Ella quickly regained her balance. Time slowed, expanding with infinite, crystalline detail. Gaia saw the fine lines etched at the sides of Ella's eyes as the woman focused on Gaia's body. She saw the pale blue veins like cool shadows on Ella's hand as she steadied the pistol for another shot. There was little chance she would miss.

Gaia coiled and sprang. Again they collided—but this time they both went tumbling to the pavement. People were staring at them now. A scream tore through the air. Obviously somebody had seen the gun. Good. That might buy Gaia a way out of this. She rolled over and shot Ella a quick glance. The woman was sprawled on the ground, flailing wildly. In her eyes Gaia saw nothing but raw rage. Ella wouldn't stop. That meant Gaia had to act. She slithered across the pavement and seized Ella's slim throat in both hands.

Ella's green eyes bulged in shock.

Gritting her teeth, Gaia pressed her thumbs into the carotid artery. This way Ella would lose consciousness in a minute. Of course, a minute was a long time when you're fighting for your life. Because Ella was struggling now, wiggling, arching her back, trying to push Gaia off. Fortunately this was one of those few times when Gaia's freakish size came in handy. She pinned Ella beneath her and continued to squeeze.

It seemed clear that there could be only one survivor.

An image of Uncle Oliver flashed into her brain, and she wondered if she would be able to hide this deed from him. But that was a consequence that couldn't stop her. Ella started to gag, her face turning purple. A faint muscle tremor signified that her muscles were starving for oxygen. But Gaia refused to let go or loosen her grip.

Without warning, Ella's gun flashed up in a blur. Gaia's left temple burst into pain. Ella had struck her with the butt of the pistol. Momentarily stunned by the blow, Gaia suddenly found their positions reversed. Ella was now straddling *her*. The woman's face was a grotesque mask of hatred and fury. Gaia stared back at her—knowing that in the next second her life would end in a vivid star burst of blood, brains, and bone.

TOM CROUCHED ON THE SIDEWALK

and withdrew his gun. Ella's back was perfectly within his sights. There was only one thing left to do. Kill her before she killed his daughter.

Ready, Aim . . .

Fire

I'LL PROBABLY GO TO JAIL FOR THIS, Ella thought, pressing the butt of the silencer against Gaia's forehead. People had seen them now. There were witnesses. But jail would be worth it in a way—

A searing pain hammered her back.

It was as if somebody had smacked her with a rod of molten iron. She slumped forward.

Unfortunately that was all Gaia needed to escape.

Not Dead Yet

FOR SOME REASON, ELLA'S CONCENTRATION wavered. Gaia lashed out with her legs and flipped the woman off her, then jumped to her feet. For a few dizzying seconds she stood there, staring down at Ella's crumpled form.

Gaia didn't understand it. How had she managed to escape? Why hadn't Ella pulled the trigger? What had stopped her? Certainly not her conscience . . .

But that was when Gaia saw the thin trickle of blood coming from Ella's fur coat, pooling in rivulets on the pavement.

Somebody shot her.

"Jesus," Ella groaned. "I think I've been shot."

Gaia's eyes flashed around the street. The few onlookers were scurrying in every direction. All but one, in fact . . . a dark figure crouched on the opposite curb and silhouetted against the reddish sun. The figure was holding a gun.

"Uncle Oliver," she whispered.

Yes. Her heart overflowed with warmth. It *was* him. His eyes bored into her own with an icy gaze.

But then Gaia's smile faltered. Something . . . something wasn't quite right. Even from this distance, even in the glare and shock and madness, she knew that those weren't the same pair of eyes into which she had gazed Monday night at dinner.

"Gaia," he called.

The voice wasn't the same, either. She stiffened. It was rougher—a voice out of the past, a voice thick with terrible memories—

"Gaia!"

It was her father.

She took a step back. Time came to a complete standstill.

"I love you," he called. "I—"

A sudden movement caught her gaze. Ella was scrambling for her gun. Gaia kicked Ella's wrist as hard as she could. Snap. The gun flew off onto the cobbled sidewalk and skidded into a sewer hole. Gaia glanced up again.

The figure was gone.

218

Gaia blinked several times. Maybe she'd just hallucinated the entire sequence of events. But *somebody* had shot Ella. Of that there was no doubt. Which meant that Gaia had to get out of here. She knew that any moment her strength would fade, her adrenaline would drain, and she would collapse. She had to get somewhere safe first.

"WHAT HAPPENED LAST NIGHT?"

It Must Be Now

Loki asked, staring out the window of his apartment at the rapidly darkening Manhattan skyline.

"A minor setback," Pearl replied from the couch. "Nothing that can't be fixed this evening."

"Please be more specific," Loki said evenly. "Given your fee, I think I'm entitled to the details."

Pearl sighed, and her tone became more businesslike. "She didn't drink all the poison—just a bare bit of it. At the last minute she remembered that she had to see her husband off, and she jumped up before she finished her glass."

Loki turned to her. "Does she suspect anything?"

"No." Pearl shook her head and smiled. "I'm sure

she woke up feeling awful today, but she drank a lot of wine last night. No doubt she'll blame that. I arranged a backup meeting for tonight, at nine. So she'll be dead by nine-thirty or so."

"Good," said Loki. "I know I can count on you."

Pearl shrugged. "That's why they pay me the big bucks," she said.

For the first time in a very long while, the future is not a bleak landscape—a harsh, barren desert defined by misery and loneliness. No. For the first time in a very long while, I have hope.

It's an emotion I haven't experienced since I was your age, my sweet.

But now, I will claim what should always have been rightfully mine. You will belong to me, Gaia, from this moment forward and forever. And the future holds wonders you can't possibly begin to imagine.

If you could glimpse what lies ahead, you might finally understand the depths of my feelings. Of course, if I told you that would someday change the course of human affairs, the course of politics—permanently, irrevocably—you might not believe me. Skepticism runs deep in our blood. Which is as it should be. Doubt is healthy. Particularly when it comes to the unimaginable.

Trust me, Gaia, all doubts

will be laid to rest. But that is
for another time . . . another
place. Far from here.

Your mother doubted me, too,
Gaia. She doubted my motives; she
doubted my very soul. To this day,
I cannot understand it. She loved
Tom—and who *is* Tom, but my mirror
image? Tom and I closer than broth-
ers; we sprung from the same cells,
the same material, the same *code*.
Whatever belongs to him belongs to
me as well. The environment alone
has shaped our differences.

That *is* the truth: we have only
external stimuli to blame for the
rift that tore us apart. The rift
that took you from me, Gaia. So in a
way, I don't blame Tom. I never did.

But I have learned from all
this. Oh, yes. I have learned
that external stimuli must be
controlled. *Censored*.

You couldn't possibly understand what I'm talking about,
Gaia. But you will. And when you
do, the two of us will be one.

here is a
sneak peek of
Fearless™
#12: KILLER

In algebra and other heinous forms of advanced math, there's a lot of talk about logic. You know—if A equals B, and B equals C, then A must equal C. Get it? That kind of thing. It's pretty obvious. I mean, you don't have to have a degree in rocket science to make these sorts of basic connections. Even somebody who hates math (like me) can grasp the old A is to B is to C bit.

So it's kind of strange that it took me so long to figure out that my father was the one who shot Ella on the street yesterday.

Okay. I guess I should back up a little. Actually, what I should do is break it down into mathematical terms. You know, show you the *logic* of it.

A) I saw my father

B) He was pointing a gun at Ella.

C) Ella got shot.

So obviously, my father was the one who shot Ella. This should have been very clear to me from the moment it happened. But still, I just couldn't bring myself to believe it. Of course, that's because the idea of my father shooting my foster mother raises a lot of very disturbing questions—the kind of questions that are about as far from logic as you can get.

For starters, what was my father even *doing* there? All of a sudden he bursts out of nowhere and saves my life.

Oh, yeah, I forgot to mention a key part of this whole equation: Ella was trying to kill me. That actually sounds a lot more shocking than it really is. Legally, she's my foster mother, but legality is about as far as the relationship goes. She's working for somebody (whom, I don't know); she's trained in martial arts (again, this is a total surprise); and, she's very unbalanced. Psychotic, in fact. (Why, I have no idea.) All I know for certain is that she hates my guts—and she has from the moment she met me.

Which brings us back to the

incident on the street.

Recently, the tension between Ella and me has been a little worse than usual. Maybe that's an understatement. If the previous tension could be represented by say, a single Krispy Kreme donut, the tension now can be represented by a donut the size of Australia. There are a lot of reasons for this, most of which revolve around a certain Sam Moon, and none of which I feel like addressing at the moment.

All I know for certain is that I can no longer live with Ella. Again, it's just a matter of logic. It doesn't make much sense to live with a woman who's trying to kill me, right?

Luckily, I have a way out.

My uncle Oliver is kidnapping me. Of course, "kidnapping" is also strictly a legal term—like "foster mother." I'll be a very willing victim. Because by kidnapping me, he'll be saving my life. Which he's already done on one occasion. It's something he and my father have in common—besides an uncanny resemblance. That's right. Coincidentally, my uncle is another blood relative who happened to explode out of nowhere and save my life. But I guess that would make sense. He and my father are twins. Why wouldn't they choose to behave in the same totally inexplicable way?

There's only one little catch. Before I leave town with my uncle—before I say good-bye to this city for the rest of my life (or at least until I turn eighteen)—I have to find my father.

Yes, I realize that this sounds stupid. I realize that it defies logic. My life is in danger. But I don't have a choice. I have to know why my father tracked me down. He has to answer for the past five years. Somebody does, anyway, because I'm sick and tired of being so confused. Anyway, I keep imagining the conversation we'll have when I do confront him.

It runs over and over again in my head, like one of those adventure-fantasy books where you choose your own ending. Mostly, it consists of me firing a lot of questions at him. (No, the gun imagery is not intentional.)

Why did he and Oliver have a falling out?

What happened between him and Oliver and my mother?

Why did he abandon me?

The list goes on, and it takes a lot of different paths, depending on how I imagine the way my father responds. Sometimes I see him falling on his knees, begging for forgiveness. Sometimes I see him turning his back on me. Sometimes he's not there at all.

The last one is the scenario that seems most likely. But this fantasy conversation probably won't even be an issue.

Especially if Ella recovers from her gunshot wound.

FEARLESS™

LET'S FACE IT, GAIA MAY HAVE BEEN
BORN WITHOUT THE FEAR GENE—BUT
YOU WEREN'T, AND TO BE A FLY FEMME
FATALE ON THE GO, YOU NEED A BAG OF
TRICKS! RIGHTING WRONGS AND
AVENGING EVIL IS A FULL TIME GIG AND
A GIRL'S GOTTA BOUNCE AT A
MOMENT'S NOTICE.

TEST YOUR *FEARLESS* TRIVIA. YOU
COULD WIN A MESSENGER BAG
JAMMED WITH ALL THE STUFF YOU
NEED TO KEEP **YOU** MOBILE—FROM
LIPSTICK TO A LAPTOP, YOU WON'T
BELIEVE WHAT'S PACKED IN HERE!

CHECK OUT WWW.ALLOY.COM FOR YOUR CHANCE TO WIN

ALLOY.com   netmarket.com ⓜ   SKYTEL   3011 (1 of 3)

FEARLESS™

OFFICIAL RULES FOR "WIN A FEARLESS MESSENGER BAG AT ALLOY.COM"

NO PURCHASE NECESSARY.

ELIGIBILITY: Sweepstakes begins August 1, 2000 and ends September 30, 2000. Entrants must be 14 years or older as of August1, 2000 and a legal U.S. resident to enter. Corporate entities are not eligible. Employees and the immediate family members of such employees (or people living in the same household) of Simon & Schuster, Inc., Alloy Online, Inc., 17th Street Productions, Netmarket Group Inc., and Skytel and their respective advertising, promotion, production agencies and the affiliated companies of each are not eligible. Participation in this Sweepstakes constitutes contestant's full and unconditional agreement to and acceptance of the Official Sweepstakes Rules.

HOW TO ENTER: No purchase necessary. To enter, visit the Alloy Web site at www.alloy.com and answer each of the Fearless trivia questions on the entry form at the site. Submit your entry by fully completing the entry form. To be eligible for the grand prize you must answer each question correctly. Eligible entries will be entered into a random drawing for the grand prize. Chances of winning the grand prize depend on the number of eligible entries received. Entries must be received by September 30, 2000, 11:59 p.m., Eastern Standard Time. There is no charge or cost to register. No mechanically reproduced entries accepted. One entry per e-mail address. Simon & Schuster, Inc., Alloy Online, Inc., Netmarket Group Inc. and Skytel and their respective agents are not responsible for incomplete, lost, late, damaged illegible or misdirected e-mail or for technical, hardware or software failures of any kind, lost or unavailable network connections, or failed, incomplete garbled or delayed computer transmissions which may limit a user's ability to participate in the Sweepstakes or any condition caused by events beyond their control which may cause this Sweepstakes to be disrupted or corrupted. All notifications in the Sweepstakes will be sent by e-mail. Sponsor is not responsible, and may disqualify you if your e-mail address does not work or if it is changed without prior notice to us via e-mail at contest@alloymail.com. Sponsor reserves the right to cancel or modify the Sweepstakes if fraud or technical failures destroy the integrity of the Sweepstakes as determined by Sponsor, in its sole discretion. If the Sweepstakes is so canceled, announced winner will receive prize to which s/he is entitled as of the date of cancellation.

RANDOM DRAWING: Prize Winner will be selected in a random drawing from among all eligible entries on October 1, 2000 to be conducted by Alloy Online designated judges, whose decisions are final. Winner will be notified by e-mail on or about October 3, 2000. Odds of winning the prize depends on the number of eligible entries received.

FEARLESS™

PRIZE: (1): A messenger bag (approx. retail value: $29.00) provided by Alloy including the following: an Apple iBook laptop computer (approx. retail value: $1,599.00), a 3Com Palm V Connected Organizer (approx. retail value: $329.00), a Diamond Multimedia MP3 Player (approx. retail value: $269.95), a Canon PowerShot S10 Digital camera (approx. retail value: $699.00) all provided by Netmarket Group Inc., a Motorola PageWriter 2000X with 1 year service plan (approx. retail value: $815.00) provided by Skytel, a pair of sunglasses, (approx. retail value: $10.00), a wallet (approx. retail value $15.00) all provided by Alloy, a Nokia 6190 wireless phone (approx. retail value: $199.00), Fearless #1 (approx. retail value $5.99), a Master combination lock (approx. retail value : $3.99), a key chain with light (approx. retail value $10.00) a Stila lipstick (approx. retail value: $25.00), and Altoids (approx. retail value $4.99) all provided by Pocket Books (approx. total retail value $4,015.00)

Prize is subject to all federal, state and local taxes, which are the sole responsibility of the winner. Prize is not transferable. No cash substitution, transfer or assignment of prize will be allowed, except by Alloy Online, Inc. in which case a prize of equal or greater value will be awarded.

GENERAL: All federal, state and local laws and regulations apply. Void in Puerto Rico and wherever prohibited. By entering, winner or if applicable winner's parent or legal guardian consents to use of winner's name by Alloy Online, Inc. without additional compensation. Entries become Alloy Online, Inc.'s property and will not be returned. For a copy of these official rules, send a self-addressed stamped envelope to Alloy 151 West 26th Street, 11th Floor, NY, NY 10001, Attn: Fearless Messenger Bag Sweepstakes Official Rules.

AFFIDAVIT OF ELIGIBILTY/RELEASE: To be eligible to win, winner will be required to sign and return an affidavit of eligibility/release of liability (except where prohibited by law). Winner under the age of 18 must have their parent or guardian sign the affidavit and release as well. Failure to sign and return the affidavit or release within 14 days, or to comply with any term or condition in these Official Rules may result in disqualification and the prize being awarded to an alternate winner. Return of any prize notification/prize as undeliverable may result in disqualification and the awarding of the prize to an alternate winner. By accepting prize, winner (or if applicable, winner's parent or legal guardian) grants Alloy Online, Inc. permission to use his or her name, picture, portrait, likeness and voice for advertising, promotional and/or publicity purposes connected with this Sweepstakes without additional compensation (except where prohibited by law).

Neither Simon & Schuster, Inc. nor Alloy Online, Inc. shall have responsibility or liability for any injury, loss or damage of any kind arising out of participation in this Sweepstakes or the acceptance or use or misuse of the prize.

WINNER: The winner's first name and state of residence will be posted at www.alloy.com on October 10, 2000 or, for the winner's name and state of residence available after October 15, 2000, send a self-addressed, stamped, #10 envelope to: Alloy 151 West 26th Street, 11th Floor, NY, NY 10001, Attn: Fearless Messenger Bag Sweepstakes.